The Lock-keeper's Wife

Also by John MacKenna

Novels

Clare

The Last Fine Summer

A Haunted Heart

The Space Between Us

Joseph

Hold Me Now

Short-Story Collections

The Fallen and Other Stories

A Year of Our Lives

The River Field

Once We Sang Like Other Men

We Seldom Talk About the Past

Memoir

Things You Should Know

Absent Friend

Non-Fiction

Castledermot and Kilkea: A Social History

Shackleton: An Irishman in Antarctica (with Jonathan Shackleton)

The Lost Village

I Knew This Place (Radio Essays)

Children's Books

Turkey's Delight

South

Poetry Collections

The Occasional Optimist

Ten Poems

Where Sadness Begins

By the Light of Four Moons

Plays

The Fallen

Who by Fire

The Unclouded Day Towards Evening

Faint Voices

Sergeant Pepper

Over the Rainbow

The Woman at the Window

My Father's Life

Redemption Song

Lucinda Sly

Between Your Love and Mine (with Leonard Cohen)

The Mental

The Lock-keeper's Wife

John MacKenna

THE LILLIPUT PRESS
DUBLIN

First published 2026 by
THE LILLIPUT PRESS
62–63 Sitric Road,
Arbour Hill,
Dublin 7,
Ireland
www.lilliputpress.ie

10 9 8 7 6 5 4 3

A CIP record for this title is available from The British Library.

Paperback ISBN 978 1 84351 972 0
eBook ISBN 978 1 84351 986 7

Set in 12 pt on 16 pt Adobe Caslon Pro and MD Lorien by Compuscript
This digitally-printed edition first produced 2026 by Lightning Source

For my dear friend Frank Taaffe

The fog wraps
the branches: ghost of field hangs
over the field . . .

Seán Hewitt, 'Psalm'

1950

Monday, May 1

Last night, on the corridor of The Mental, I met the book-keeper, a man who hadn't spoken a word to me in the six weeks he'd been there. He stopped and said: 'I believe you're leaving us tomorrow.'

'I am,' I said.

'I don't know if you remember,' he said, 'but the first night I was here, I was sitting in the dining room. You wouldn't have known it but the words and the sadness were flying around my head like bats on a twilit road and then you came and sat beside me and, more than anything, I wanted to put my hand on yours and to feel the warmth of your skin, the outline of the bones beneath that skin, the contours of your fingers and the possibility of their twining with mine.'

'I remember,' I said.

'Thank you,' he said.

And then he walked away.

There are men who are wise. I have met some in my life. My father is one. And there was a man who lived close to Mullaghcreelan Woods, an old man who needed no one's company beyond his own, who had a wisdom and a way with a few words and a memory that astounded me each time we spoke. The book-keeper had a wisdom about him, even in his silence. I knew that before ever he spoke and then I heard it in his voice and in the words he used. I will never forget the way he talked about those bats on the twilit road.

I wish we had spoken more but it was almost time for me to leave The Mental.

My husband is not a wise man; he's a fool and worse.

My husband sent a hackney car to collect me. He wouldn't come himself, of course. He didn't bring me to The Mental and he wouldn't collect me, and, if you asked him, he'd slobber at you over his drink that he *didn't have the heart for it*, couldn't bear to see me *put away* in that place. Sometimes he gets his tongue around a word like *incarcerated* and it makes him feel like a great fellow.

In the three months I was there, he never once darkened the door or travelled the twenty miles to see me.

So there I was, standing in the hallway, my bag at my feet, watching the avenue for a sign of the hackney car. It was very early, but it was bright. Summer had arrived that first May morning.

My husband had written and told me the car would come early, *to give you a start on the day and the new life*, but what that really meant was to get me home before most people were up and about.

I sat in the passenger seat and heard the boot bang closed and then the driver sat in beside me. I didn't know him and he didn't know me. Another precaution by my husband. The story he put about was that I had gone back home to Moone to mind my father. As if anyone believed that; as if anyone knows or cares where I go or what I am.

'Well,' the driver asked, smiling over at me, 'are we right for the road?'

His smile was sincere.

'We are,' I said.

'You'll be glad to be getting out of here?'

I nodded but I wondered if going back was the right thing to do.

He started the engine and swung the car around on the gravelled drive. As he did, I saw two men cycling up the avenue. One was dressed in a guard's uniform and the other had a suitcase tied on the carrier of his bike. They cycled past us, heads down.

Every time I'd watched someone come or go from that place, I'd thought about my father and myself cycling the hill up to Bolton and then down the long run into Moone. Often, in those rememberings, we were cycling to a football match in Athy or to catch a train to a match in Dublin and he was encouraging me with every turn of the wheel and every stand on the pedal: 'Good girl yourself, you're a topper.'

Friday, May 19

Along the riverbank the whitethorn has cut loose from its buds and spouted into blossom. When I walk there in the morning and the evening, I notice a change in shade. The morning light on the dew that hangs in the flowers is full of gaudy things, like marbles in a tin basin. The flowers say *look at me*, as if they need to say anything to attract attention. By evening they have settled down. That childish burst of need is gone; they have had the sunlight of the day, they are calm before the sleep of night and, even when the dew or the rain have fallen on them, they shine with a different light.

Sometimes I think of myself now and myself in girlhood and I see a parallel with the whitethorn. Back then, when first I went to work in Waterford, I needed people to see me, I needed to be heard. I craved people's attention and wanted them to know that, even though I was only a shop girl, I was intelligent and could hold a conversation.

I remember the shop manager, a harridan, saying once: 'Miss McDermot, the more you talk, the less you sell.'

'I'm sorry, Mrs James,' I said, by way of explanation. 'I was just trying to be friendly with the customers.'

'Miss McDermot, the more you talk, the less you sell,' she said again.

'I understand, Mrs James. I was just thinking that if I talked to people they might buy more.'

'Miss McDermot, the more you talk, the less you sell.'

I might have gone on arguing my point but one of the other girls kicked me hard and I shut up.

The fields that rise and fall on either side of the river and canal are full of the ticking clocks of dandelions. When the wind lifts, the seconds and minutes of their seeds rise in the air like there is no tomorrow and sail away across the fields and over the ditches into other fields and

I think about next spring and next summer and hope I remember this day when I see the fields full of yellowness again.

Sometimes I start to run along the bank, my hand brushing the branches of the trees and bushes that lean out to form a kind of lazy arch above the path. And sometimes I feel like a child, running for the sheer pleasure of it, and sometimes I feel like I'm a woman running for my life, my small, short life.

I remember thinking, one evening last week, that there's a time between the fall of the cherry blossom and the fall of the May bush when everything is poised, one set of flowers gone for another year, one waiting for their end. And I had this sense that, when my own time comes, it will be in the days between the tumbling of the cherry blossom and the dropping of the whitethorn.

I had this vision of my last breath being expelled somewhere along this very path, my eyes closing finally on the world, my body and my soul fallen with the flowers of April and May. And I felt a sense of happiness. I had no fear of dying. I saw myself lying in the long grass beside the worn towpath. I wasn't curled like a sleeping child. My arms were spread above my head, my dress was laid across my body like a mass of wildflowers, and I knew one of the bargemen would find me and think I was sleeping. He'd cough and clear his throat to wake me, then realise, as he drew nearer, that I was, indeed, asleep, and this time for ever.

Sunday, May 21

The swallows have come home again.

When I was in The Mental, I used to think about them. On cold March afternoons, I'd walk around the garden and try to avoid the other patients, try to find a corner beneath the thirty-foot wall, a place where a sliver of sun and the shelter of a tree would allow me to pretend it was summer, that I was free, that everything would be all right.

I thought, if the swallows can get back here from Africa, then I can make myself well enough to get out of The Mental. If they can fly thousands of miles to be here in summer, I can make my own little journey.

And so I'd stand in the finger of light that came like the finger of a god from heaven and I'd close my eyes and suck every ounce of heat from the day and imagine myself on this riverbank, watching the swallows loop and dive and rise and fall in search of food, and I'd be happy in the belief that I could do that, too. Get back to a place where I had some small sense of belonging.

The thought of getting truly home, back to Moone, to my father and the neighbours I knew and the fields and woods where I had grown up, was not something I ever allowed myself to imagine.

Another time, I saw a patient having a fit in the corridor of the hospital and I went and wrote about it, about him, but really I was thinking about the swallows on the Barrow bank, the sky gone epileptic with the madness of their joy.

Wednesday, May 24

Hesitation and *murmuration*, those are today's two words.

It's as if the May bushes have frozen or hesitated. They've been on the brink of flowering for a week now, the buds ripe and ready, but everything seems to be petrified, as if they're waiting for someone or something to give a signal. Each morning I walk the bank of the river and expect them to have emerged with the sun, but each morning I'm met with the same, arrested buds, still curled about themselves.

On the road this afternoon, cycling back from town, I stopped to watch a small murmuration of starlings over the field beyond the pump. Each time they turned in the sun, they disappeared, and then they'd turn again and reappear. Appear and disappear. Appear and disappear. There and gone. There, then lost in the sun. There, then gone for good, lost behind the line of sycamores.

Friday, May 26

I met my husband at a railway station. On the platform of the station in Maganey. I was catching a train back to Waterford and he was catching the same train but travelling only as far as Bagenalstown. It was a Sunday afternoon. The sun was still high in the sky and the station was quiet. We were the only two people on the platform. Now and then the station foreman would appear and disappear in the doorway of the ticket office.

There were four milk churns at the end of the platform and a basket with what sounded like ducks inside. Otherwise, the afternoon was still. Now and then a wagtail would land and peck his way between the rails, then take to the air again.

My future husband spoke first. 'You're waitin' for the train?'

I should have known, from that one question, that almost everything about him would be predictable.

'I am,' I said without turning.

'Travellin' far?'

'Waterford.'

'Do you live there?'

'I work there.'

'So where's home?'

So many questions.

'A Civic Guard wouldn't ask me that,' I said, turning to face him.

It was then that his waistcoat caught my attention. It was multi-coloured, like no waistcoat I had ever seen before. It reminded me of the kingfishers I'd see skating over the waters of the river Griese on a summer day.

'I'm sorry. I was just wonderin'.'

'Near Moone. Beyond Castledermot.'

'It sounds like a quiet place. I like quiet places.'

And then he introduced himself. Told me he was a lock-keeper on the canal. He had been to Castledermot to visit a friend of his who had been injured in a farming accident and had lost the use of his legs.

'I like your waistcoat,' I said.

'The brightest thing about me.'

I should have listened.

We shared a compartment on the train, just the two of us, the windows open, the leather window straps struggling in the summer wind as the train sped to Carlow and on to Bagenalstown. By then he had asked for my name and address and promised to write, if I didn't mind.

As he stepped down from the train, he said, 'I'll write this very evening.'

It was probably the most compulsive thing he would ever say or do.

And there it was, on the Tuesday morning: a letter beside my plate on the dining table in the boarding house.

'Looks interesting,' one of the girls laughed. 'Not your father's handwriting.'

The only letters that ever came were from my father.

'Come on, who is he?' someone else asked.

I read the letter. It was short and to the point. *I'll be in Waterford on Sunday next. My train gets in at the Angelus time of the morning. I'll meet you at the clock on the cay at half past twelve, if you want to. I'll wait there until two of the clock. If you don't turn up by then I'll know.*

I turned up. Mostly, I think, because Sundays were tedious and I wanted to see the waistcoat again.

The second or third time he came to visit me, I took him on the bus to Tramore and we walked together along the beach.

‘There’s nothing like the sea for power and beauty,’ I said.

‘Sure what’s the sea but a hape of rivers?’ he said.

I should have listened.

That was the summer of 1926. We were married in the summer of 1928. I was twenty-two and he was twenty-eight and, if I ask myself the question now, I have no idea why I married him.

As we left the room where people were dancing on the evening of our wedding, my father said: ‘If you’re not happy, you can leave him. Don’t worry what people might say. You’ll always have a home in Moone.’

And now there are kingfishers along this stretch of river, small parcels of water that lift from the river and hoist with them every colour in creation. They fly on, low and fast, and then they’re gone into the evening or the morning light. Low and fast between the bursting willows, melting back into whatever world it is they’ve come here from.

Saturday, June 3

I walked up this morning through the Little Wood at the top of the hill. The grass was still wet from the dew and everywhere I went my feet left impressions that followed me between the trees.

I caught sight of a fox, late home, disappearing through a gap in a hedge. There, then gone, then rusty red again, then gone again. The natural world is full of magical creatures appearing and disappearing.

The bluebells were like low, slow smoke on the floor of the wood, like something imagined, like the ghosts of children's faces in the summer moon.

Sunday, June 4

There were forty-seven people at early Mass in the little church this morning. My husband goes to second Mass in the big church in the town and comes back home at four or five in the afternoon, his bicycle weaving its own way from the pub to the house, past people walking on the riverbank. I wish he'd fall in and drown, dragged down by the weight of the bike when there's no one about to rescue him. I imagine bubbles rising like angels in his wake, glad to see the back of him, and then *peace, perfect peace*, like you see carved on the Protestant headstones.

Forty-seven people in the church. I knelt at the front of the gallery and counted them. Three others on the gallery: the postmistress, the teacher in the country school and the man who mends the bicycles. That's four of us.

The priest and two altar servers on the altar. That's seven.

On one side there's the retired Civic Guard, his wife, their son who never did a day's work in his life and their daughter who leaves their house only for Mass. The cobbler who tried to get me to kiss him in exchange for not charging me for re-soling my husband's boots. 'Why don't you get my husband to kiss you?' I told him.

The woman with the red hair who lives out beyond the next island on the river and her seven children who all have different hair and different looks and clothes that are never right, clothes they never quite grow into or seem always to have just grown out of. That's twenty.

On the other side there's the woman dressed in black and I'm always wondering why and I've never found out. There's the man who owns the shop that no one goes into because of the boycott thirty years ago. The people won't go in and he won't shut the doors but they'll all turn out for his funeral and say 'He wasn't the worst in the world'. There's the two brothers and their two wives and their six children between them who all live in the one house at the end of the Mill Lane where there is no mill and hasn't been for two hundred years. There's the tailor with one hand, the railway man with the bent leg, the ploughman with half a head of hair and the woman with the odd eye and they all sit on the same bench Sunday after Sunday, as if they're not allowed to sit anywhere else, as if they're happier together in a freak show. There's the two brothers from the farm up the hill. There's The Cowboy, so called because he won a calf in a raffle twenty years ago and sold it for half a crown so that he could go to the pictures in Carlow. That's thirty-nine.

And then there's the seven women who kneel on the stone floor at the back. The Vestal Virgins people call them. Seven widows from the wars. Three from the war just over: Mag Kane, Mary Langton and Annie Kernahan. And four from the War of Independence. Was there ever a war that gave us women less independence? Rosie Loughran, Babs Burke, Honoria Kelly and Sheila Sammon. They call Sheila *The Sammon of Knowledge.*

And there, in the doorway to the side, is The Man in the Cap. He appears every Sunday after the first prayers and leaves the minute communion is over. No one seems to know who he is. He never receives communion and never removes his cap. There and gone.

Forty-seven of us all in one small church and each one as daft, or dafter, than the next, but I'm the only one who's been inside the gates and doors of The Mental.

Friday, June 23

St John's Eve.

When I was a young girl, the summer before I left home to work in the shop in Waterford, my father took me walking. It was as if he thought he'd never see me again, that he had things to say, wisdom to impart, and there might never be another time in which to do it.

He told me about St John's Eves when he was a boy and I said they sounded like times from a thousand years ago.

'And sure maybe it is a thousand years ago,' he said, 'or maybe two thousand years ago. The Lord alone knows. Will I tell you more?'

'Do.'

'Well, where I come from, a bonfire had to be lit at the very minute the sun slipped below the hills and it had to be kept lighting till the last minute of the day. And the old people would pray that the harvest would be good and the fields would produce strong crops and the weather would be clement.'

'Only the old people?'

'The rest of us would be busy. There'd be music playing and people would be dancing and there'd be fellows wrestling and running races by the light from the bonfire. My mother always prayed that the fields would give crops to keep my father in work and that the garden at the back of our house would give enough food to keep us fed. But the younger people cared nothing for wishes like that. Some boyos would jump into the river, believing a swim on St John's Eve was a protection again drowning for the rest of the year.'

'And was it?'

'I seen too many young fellows and girls dragged out of the river over the years to believe that but, sure, who am I to know?'

'Go on,' I said. I didn't want my father to be haunted by the ghosts of the drowned in his dreams or in his waking memories.

'People used to throw weeds into the fire in the hope that their like wouldn't grow in the fields. And fellows would challenge one another to lep the flames. That kind of thing. And then in the small hours, when the fire had died down, people would take some of the ashes and spread it in fields and gardens to encourage the growth of the crops. They were different times, *leanbh*, different times.'

'Did you ever lep the fire?'

'Indeed and I did.'

'And did other things like that happen?'

'Oh, they did. There was a man near us and his house was built on a fairy path – never a good place to build, people said. So every St John's Eve he'd bring home coals from the fire and keep them burning on the path till daylight and that warded off the fairies and other strange travellers.' My father paused at that point. 'Or so he said.'

'You didn't believe it worked?'

'Well, the thing about people not drowning in the river didn't work so why would the coals? And, to tell you the truth, I've never in my fifty years and more seen sight nor light of a fairy or even the leavings of one!'

But today there are no fires burning, not even in the grate of this house. The day is too hot and the sky too blue and the wind too warm for fires. And today I'm only ten years younger than my father was when he told me that story of the other times, when he was a boy, a story of the world that has gone for ever.

'The other world disappeared with the coming of the radio,' my father used to say. 'There's no heaven and no hell since the radio arrived. Everything is real now.'

Perhaps the real world is where we find ourselves when we're sheltering from the possibility of happiness or heartbreak. I think the real world is where we survive and the rest is simply the chance that there might be something more.

Saturday, June 24

The song thrushes in the apple trees were up to greet the dawn today. They woke me and, when I opened the window to hear them more clearly, they rose, like a cloud into the mist of morning, and then settled again to their singing in the branches.

Something in the colour of the morning reminded me of the colour of my wedding frock, a whiteness but not a whiteness, and then I remembered the beer stain that is tattooed into it for ever, my husband whirling me round the floor of the hotel bar-room, a glass of stout in one hand, the other wrapped about my waist, the beer flying through the air and slopping on the back of the brand new dress one of the shop girls in Waterford had made for me, his blotched face leering and laughing, and in that moment I had an inkling that I had made a huge mistake in marrying him.

But when he took me back here, the August damsons and apples were heavy on the trees in the garden. After he had carried my cases and my little box of books upstairs, he took my hand and led me outside and we walked in the well-tilled garden beside the house.

'Every lock-keeper's house has two apple trees and two plum trees,' he told me, pointing to the trees at the other end of the triangle of garden. 'They come with the house and the house comes with the job and the job comes with me.'

He seemed delighted with the tale he was telling, as if he had been waiting all his life for this moment, as if every day of work he had done, every lock key he had turned, every groaning lock-gate that had opened and closed for him, was a step towards this conversation, and in that moment the spilling beer and red-blotched face were forgotten and I loved him again and I was filled with hope and an eagerness for the life I imagined we might have together.

We stood at the side of the lock basin and he explained how the gates opened and closed, how the rising or falling water took the barges up or down.

'It's like raising the dead or burying the dead, depending on which way the barge is travelling,' he said. 'You'll see for yourself when the next barge comes.'

And I did and for the rest of that summer and into the autumn every time a barge arrived I went and helped, or stood and watched, and week by week I got to know the bargemen and they brought me little gifts as they got to know me – a pencil or a bottle of ink or a copybook.

'I don't believe I've ever seen you come out of that house without a book in your hand or ink on your fingers or a pencil stuck into your hair like a comb,' one of them told me once and his words were like a confirmation to me.

'That'll be the habit from shop work,' I said.

'Well, I doubt you're running a shop beyond in the house,' the bargeman said, laughing. 'The boss-man tells me you're a great one for the books and the writing.'

There were times when my husband was away, when I'd open and shut the lock gates, sell them soda bread or scones I'd made, share a mug of tea with the bargemen as their craft rose or fell, listen to their stories of ghosts on the water and unexplained lights in the depths and voices grumbling in the night as the barges moved slowly through the darkness. Stories of the barge horses refusing to pass places where women had drowned, the bargemen having to coax them along, sacks thrown over the horses' heads to blinker them from whatever it was they were seeing.

On autumn days I loved to stand by the lock basin and listen to the roar of the wind in the trees, the breeze sweeping over the face of the water, the draught catching my hair and lifting it into the air. The world seemed fresh and new and something downstream offered the promise of the bright, the undiscovered, of another way of life.

I knew that the river became the sea at Waterford. I had worked there, never dreaming I would one day live on the bank of this waterway that helped to feed the ocean. Never knowing that there were places – like the one in which I now lived – where it was necessary for boats and barges to leave the full flow of the river and enter the quieter, gentler waters of the canal. Places where the roar of the water became noiseless and the only sound was the growl of the wind in the trees on autumn days

Monday, June 26

Last night I had the strangest dream. When we were first married, my husband and I would share our dreams in the light of morning. And, sometimes, if there were no dreams to share, we'd tell stories of our childhoods. Later, when my husband had grown tired of storytelling and told me it was time to put *all that ould rubbish behind us*, I'd share dreams with the children, building stories into and around the visions of the night. And then, when they were grown and gone, I stopped remembering my dreams. But last night a dream found its way into my sleep and, for once, I've remembered it.

In the dream, I was walking in the woods at Mullaghcreelan. It was a summer evening, that time of day when everything falls silent, the minutes just before darkness materialises. I was walking down the long avenue and the ground was hard and dusty from weeks without rain. And then I met myself, a girl of seventeen, and beside me, or her, was a long-dead dog I'd had as a girl.

The first thing I noticed about myself was that my eyes were hazelnut brown, even in the late evening, in the falling dusk; they shone with the light of youth and hope and excitement and anticipation. And the air was full of the scent of bluebells, heavy and sweet but not cloying. A slight breeze lifted the perfume of the flowers, dropped it and lifted it again. It was there and gone and there again.

I recognised myself immediately and I knew – even in the mad world that is dreams – that there was something strange about meeting myself and a dog who had been buried years before. The dog was a bearded collie, given to my father by a Scotsman on whose farm he'd worked for a couple of years. His name was Jock – a beautiful, gentle, shambling dog. My father always said that he'd been given the dog because it refused to herd sheep.

'Why would it?' he'd said. 'Sheep, like cows, are more than capable of herding themselves.'

And here was Jock again, faithful as ever by my side, ambling through the last light of evening, stopping to smell the bluebells every so often. And then the younger me began to hurry along the rising path, coming swiftly towards the older me, and the dog fell in beside her, matching her stride for stride, eager not to lose or be lost by his mistress.

I wondered why they were suddenly anxious to be elsewhere. I wanted to enquire but as the younger me passed, and before I could speak, she smiled and hurried away through the trees. The dog ignored me, as though I were the ghost and he the living creature. I raised a hand in greeting but there was no response, no recognition beyond that cursory smile.

And in this dream I was shaken by the fact that time had driven us apart, this young woman and me; I was saddened by the long-lost dog and his not paying me the slightest heed, and saddened that my heart did not know then the things I know now. I wanted so much to tell the young Julie McDermot of the lessons I had learned, to make the way ahead a little clearer and a little easier for her. I turned to follow, thinking I could catch her up, but as I did, she disappeared into the dusk, the dog still bounding at her heels, his tail swishing with the pleasure of their hurried walk. And then she was gone and I woke with that awful gnawing sense of what is lost and what can never be undone and I knew I would never see her again.

Tuesday, June 27

Today is my daughter Margaret's birthday. She's twenty years of age. I posted her a letter last week with a ten-shilling note inside. How that'll work out for her in London I have no idea but there'll be some way of changing it in a post office.

She was born on a Friday. I called her Margaret, after my mother, but my husband always called her Betty, out of spite, I think, because I didn't call her Dorothy after his mother.

She was always a sensible child. I never had to worry about her going too near the water. And she was good in school and she was good at home. When the dark days came for me, she was the one who got herself and her brother off to school. She was the one who made the lunches and packed them in the school bags. She was the one who made sure the homework lessons were done in the evenings.

And she was sensible enough to fly away when she could and to bring her younger brother with her. The pair of them took the boat from Dun Laoghaire to Holyhead in the first week of January that seems more years ago than it really is. There was nothing for them here, beyond their father telling them they should have jobs. As if jobs grow on trees. Telling them, for the umpteenth time, that staying on in school was the worst thing they ever did.

'If youse had got jobs when youse were fourteen, youse'd be well up the ladder now, instead of walkin' around knockin' on doors that'll never be opened. There's such a thing as being too well educated. No one wants a smart arse workin' for them.'

So off they went, Margaret and Robert. I wished them well, encouraged them to leave. I told them there was nothing here for them. They're only children still. Well, Robert is – eighteen going on twelve – but Margaret has her head screwed on. She's working in a shop, just like her mother. And Robert has a job in a hotel. She keeps an eye on him. They meet on Sundays and once or twice during the week. She's talking of going to night classes come September.

I love the memory of my children. The way they were when they were small. The picnics that the three of us would have along the bank or in the High Field, up in the shadow of the chestnut with the breeze blowing down from the Ridge to cool the day. And the cows lying in the shelter of trees in fields along the lane. I miss those days but those days were gone anyway and I don't begrudge the pair of them their freedom. If anything, I envy them their youth and all the possibilities that lie before them.

On the way back from the High Field, we'd pass the River Field and we'd stop at the gate and sit on the top bar and I'd look across at the corner and the outline of the stones in the rich grass and I'd smile at the thought that there might have been four of them here with me, rather than two.

Sunday, July 2

I didn't go to Mass this morning. Instead, I left home at the usual time but I cycled in the opposite direction to the church. My husband was still asleep when I left, so I gathered strawberries from the garden and put them carefully in a small box on the carrier of the bike.

The morning was fine, the sky clear and I was ahead of the day. I didn't cycle through Carlow town. Instead, I took the road out to Maganey and then across to Mullaghcreelan and out onto the Moone road at Castledermot. I saw very few people until I got to the pump at Hallahoise, near Lambes' house. Jim Lambe was there, filling a bucket of water, and we talked for a while.

'You're living astray down the country now?' he said.

'Out beyond Bagenalstown.'

'And how does that suit you?'

'It's not home.'

'And have you a family itself?'

'A boy and a girl. Working beyond in London.'

'Nothing here for them,' he said.

'No.'

'Tell your father I was asking after him.'

'I will.'

'You have your drink there,' Jim said. 'I have all day to fill this bucket.'

I cupped my palms while he moved the pump handle carefully up and down, the water running slow and cold. I drank deeply, thanked him and then cycled away.

Freewheeling down the gradual fall into Castledermot, I thought of what he'd asked. Had I family? Two in London. Two in a corner of a field near the house but no one ever talks about the children buried in the fields or the grounds of ruined churches or in the fairy raths. They talk about the little people, as if there are fairies living in the shadows of the old thorn trees. But I think of the little people who are buried there, the infants who breathed for a minute or two or less. No one ever talks about them. They go unrecognised, unspoken of, but not forgotten.

And then I'm out on the road for Moone and the morning sun is still climbing and a small wind lifts my hair and cools me and I set my face for home.

My father is in his garden, picking redcurrants, when I arrive at the house. He looks up as I swing through the gateway and a smile creases his face. He could be twenty years younger than his eighty years. His skin is fresh and tanned, his mop of white hair sits like a protection from the sun.

'Well, girleen, you're a sight for sore eyes.'

Inside the house, we prepare dinner together. There are new potatoes, cabbage and ham. I pour strawberries into a basin and run cold water over them.

'They look good enough to eat,' my father says and he laughs at his own joke.

We have our meal in the cool kitchen. The door is open onto the soft chuckling of pigeons and the sharp, short shadow of box-hedge and sycamore. Many people describe sycamores as weeds. My father says they're the finest trees – sturdy, reliable, fast-growing and shelter from the wind and sun.

'I met Jim Lambe at Hallahoise. He says hello.'

'A decent man. How is he?'

'He's well.'

'I haven't seen him this long time.'

We finish our dinners and I spoon the strawberries into two bowls and leave some in the basin for my father to have later.

'There's a drop of cream in the blue jug in the shed beyont. I took it off the milk this morning. Something must have told me you were bringing these.'

In the dark, cool shed, I open the door of the safe, high on the wall, its wired sides cool to the touch, and lift the small blue jug from the bottom shelf. The handle is cold. I stand a moment and breathe deeply the reassuring childhood smell of turf. A line I read somewhere comes into my head. *How beautiful thou art.*

After we've eaten the strawberries and cream, my father asks if I'd like tea.

'Later,' I say. 'I'd like to walk to the graveyard.'

'Of course. Would you like me to come with you or would you rather go alone?'

'I'd love you to come with me.'

We walk down the hill and follow the road to the right, past Maloney's garage and down to the field of stones where my mother is laid. The grave is clean, the grass short, flowers growing at the foot of her headstone. My father visits every day. I read the words and dates on the stone.

In loving memory of
Margaret McDermot
Died December 24th 1919
Aged 39
Rest in Peace

I was thirteen then. I was sent down to the neighbours that Christmas Eve morning. For the previous two days my mother had screamed and cried and begged not to die. The neighbours passing on the road blessed themselves and hurried on, not wanting us to think they were intruding. In the end, my father told me to go down to Murphys' and stay there until he sent for me.

At four o'clock, as night was falling, word came that I was to go home. Ann Murphy walked back with me. When we rounded the corner above Maloney's, it was the silence that told me.

'God rest her,' my father said. 'She has peace at last.'

Walking to the house, my father talks about the Spanish flu.

'They say it killed five million people. I know four that died from it, apart from your mother.'

'She was afraid of death.'

'Aren't we all?'

'I suppose.'

'We're right to be, girleen. Life is all we have.'

In the kitchen, my father swings the kettle onto the range, throws in a handful of turf and opens the damper. While I set the table, he takes half a currant cake from a tin on the dresser.

'Never a week goes by that Ann Murphy doesn't drop me in a cake or a tart.'

We sit and eat.

'Are you well?' my father asks.

'I am.'

'I'm glad. That was no place to be, but if it made you better, it was the best place to be.'

I lean my chin on my palm and look at my father. I smile. I feel the brightness of his love lighting up my eyes. 'I'm well.'

He came, every Saturday, to visit me in The Mental. Always there in the big hall with a smile on his face; always chatting to patients while he waited for me to arrive. He'd keep the best side out while we walked the grounds, but I'd know. I'd see, as he cycled back down the avenue, the way his shoulders would sag and he'd have the gimp of a man that was twenty years older than his age.

But now he's smiling and I'm smiling.

'And Margaret and Robert is doing well in England?'

'Very well.'

'Good, good.' He hesitates. 'And this place is always here for you. You know that?'

'I do,' I say.

And then he changes the subject. 'Do you remember the day we took the train from Maganey to the city to see Kildare play Dublin in Jones' Road?'

'I do.'

'What age were you then?'

'I was fifteen.'

'That was a day!'

'It was.'

I don't remind him of the two Dublin men we passed on Dorset Street. They heard our country accents and one turned to the other and said, 'Do you get a fierce smell of shite?'

'Must be from the sheep-shaggers,' the other man said and I felt my face redden with anger. My father hadn't heard the remark or, if he had, he'd chosen to ignore it.

Going back, in the early evening, I cycle through Carlow, past the high, grimy walls of The Mental. They seem so much higher from the outside. I think about what led me there in the first place. How my husband found me one morning, late in January, standing naked on the bank of the river. How he told me to get dressed, for God's sake, and what did I think I was at. I said there was no God. He asked was I mad. I told him I probably was. The next thing I saw were the doctor and the priest running down the bank, cajoling me to think about my children, to think about the fact that I would be damned if I took my own life, to think about my husband, to think about my father. That's when I turned my back on them and, suddenly, they grabbed me and hoisted me up between them, like a bullock being pulled from the bog, and marched me back to the house and wrapped me up in blankets. There was talk between the doctor and my husband outside the door. The priest sat with me and asked if there was anything I needed to tell him.

'Not a thing,' I said.

'If you'd done it, Margaret, you couldn't have been buried in consecrated ground.'

'I wasn't contemplating doing anything and, anyway, neither were my two children buried in consecrated ground, Father.'

'I'm sorry. Where are they buried?'

'Above in the River Field, where the two lines of stones are.'

'Would you like me to pray there?'

I looked at him. He was only a young fellow, not long out of the college, and I hadn't the heart to tell him it was too late, to tell him my two living children were free and all I wanted was to find a way to follow them to freedom. 'If you'd like, Father.'

And, in a while, a guard came and there was more talk outside the door and, in the heel of the hunt, I was carted off to The Mental in Carlow and people were told I'd gone to Moone to look after my father for a while.

Back at the house, my husband is snoring in the armchair beside the window. A smell of beer fills the kitchen. I take my book and sit on the bench beside the lock. The sun eases itself down behind the trees on the opposite bank.

I bring in a basket of turf from the shed and then I stand at the kitchen door and watch the sun sink and wonder why I go to Mass at all.

I don't believe in a merciful, all-forgiving God because I have never seen his mercy and I have no interest in his forgiveness, nor do I believe I need it. They'd lock me up for that, too.

I don't miss Mass when I'm not there. So why do I go? After a while I decide it's because I enjoy the company of that lunatic gathering. Those people make me feel I'm not alone. I am comforted by their discomfort with the world.

Friday, July 7

Today is my son's nineteenth birthday. Robert, I wish you love and life and happiness and the willingness to take your time before you commit that life to any one person and any one road. Be patient, my beloved son.

Tuesday, July 11

I imagine Margaret making her way to work in London. In her letters, she tells me the summer there is very hot. She says the heat piles up like cocks of hay between the buildings and it gets so close sometimes it's hard to breathe. She says her brother and herself miss me but they'll never come back. I tell her she's right. She says if her father died, she wouldn't come back for his funeral. I tell her she's right in that, too.

What I don't tell her and never will is that she was conceived a month to the night after her sister died. The clay was still a tiny wound in the grass at the side of the field and her father was drunk. Crying for his lost child, he said. Broken-hearted, he said. But not too broken-hearted.

He might as well have said: 'No point in hanging round; we might as well just get on with it.'

But that's not what he said.

He said nothing at all in those moments. Just pushed himself inside, where her sister had been a few weeks before. Through the bedroom window the sky was clear and frozen and the early frost that hid the grass had hardened the clay that wrapped her sister in the earth.

Sunday, July 16

While my husband was at Mass, I made a picnic for myself and packed it in a bag and set off walking. I walked three locks down and then cut out onto the riverbank.

I kept walking until I could walk no further, until I had gone miles beyond the point where summer Sunday walkers take their strolls.

And then I found a quiet place beneath a chestnut tree and I spread my picnic on the ground and ate and drank slowly and thought about Margaret and Robert. And I thought about my father. I didn't think about the other two or about my husband. I thought only of hopeful things.

After I'd finished eating, I sat with my back against the trunk of the chestnut. A summer shower came and went but I stayed there, reading. At five o'clock I had another bite to eat and drank the last of the tea from the flask. And then I set off for home.

It was past eight o'clock when I stepped into the garden. I caught sight of him in the field behind the house. He was on his knees in the wet grass between the stones that marked the graves. I could tell by the tilt of his shoulders that he was crying. Was that for himself or for the children, I wondered. The tears were certainly not for me.

Saturday, July 29

Today my husband took a train from Bagenalstown to Kildare and from there to Thurles to visit his dying uncle.

'You never know,' he said. 'He has a big farm and no children. You never know. It's worth the price of the train journey.'

There are no working barges coming through, so the lock is quiet.

'If there's boats, holiday boats, you can see them through,' he said.

I nodded.

I gave the house a quick tidy. I know I'm not a great keeper of a kitchen but, since Margaret and Robert emigrated there's less to do and more time to do it.

When he was gone, I sat in the doorway and breathed a deep sigh of relief. He won't be back until tomorrow night. A gentle rain was falling and then the sky began to turn and the rain stopped and the clouds softened and then disappeared and by midday it was bright and hot.

I walked to the top of the River Field and spoke to the children, laid a bunch of dog daisies and poppies on each grave. The stones around the graves were clean and bright after the rain, the light catching them like the glow of coals in winter. I told them how much I loved them and how I missed them and how I hoped their lives inside me had been happy.

Do I think they're in Limbo? I do not.

If my husband's mad dream came true and his uncle left him land and we moved, would we bring the children with us or would we leave their bones there in the corner of the field, under the sorrel leaves and clover? I doubt I could go without them but it wouldn't concern him.

In the afternoon, to celebrate my two days of freedom, I cycled towards Kilkenny. Somewhere, on a back road I'd never travelled before, I passed a cottage garden and on the post beside the gate was a handwritten sign that read *Please Call.* I cycled on but the words on the sign refused to let me go, so I stopped and cycled back the way I'd come and laid my bicycle against the dense hedge beside the gate.

The bushes were high on either side of the gate but, leaning over it, I could see a cottage buried in a garden of tremendous growth. There were bean blossoms that set the sky on fire; sunflowers and hollyhocks tipped the flaking walls of a rusting shed.

I ventured up the gravelled path that lost and found and lost itself again, meandering between bright bordered marigolds, blue lupins, forget-me-nots and lavender; aubretia spilled out to carpet where I walked and there were roses round the door, wild climbing roses that seemed to hold the cottage walls together.

And then an old man appeared from a tin-roofed shed. He smiled and raised his hat.

'You called,' he said.

'I saw your sign.'

'Most people do but very few believe it.'

'I love your garden.'

'Thank you. Have you time for a cup of tea? I was about to make one.'

'That'd be lovely. Thank you.'

'Make yourself at home – have a look around the garden. It runs up the back there.'

And it did, a wildness of roses, with a path that wound its way between them and then, on a rising site, a terraced vegetable garden of potatoes, peas, beans and cabbages under nets and a hedge of redcurrant and gooseberry bushes on the highest level.

We sat outside, at a weathered wooden table. Sunlight forced its way through every crevice in the candled chestnut leaves above us.

'The garden isn't mine,' the old man said. 'It was left me by whoever lived here in the past. But what they couldn't leave was the knowledge as to who was who about these parts.'

'And so the sign?'

'And so the sign.'

'And has it worked?'

'Oh, people call and some of them stay a while but most of all they talk too much and sometimes I can't wait to see them go, yet I'm loath to take the sign down. It's part and parcel of the place by now and who knows what changes removing it might bring?'

Inside, the kettle whistled and he rose, returned with shining mugs and rhubarb tart and placed the steaming teapot between us. We ate and drank and then sat in the silence of that noisy day – bees, birds and heat were busy at their toil – for a long, long time.

Afterwards, when I got up to go, he said: 'Thank you for calling and, please, do call again.'

He walked me to the gate, I heaved my bicycle from the hedge.

'Travelling far?' he asked.

'As far as the day will take me.'

'Thank you, again, for calling and for settling with the silence.'

I stopped where the road crested the hill. Before me was a valley and beyond it lay a wood.

I turned, looked back. The old man was still standing inside his gate.

I raised my hand and waved and he waved back from the shadow of the hedge.

Monday, July 31

My husband came back late last night.

'That bastard could hang on for months,' he said. 'But, anyway, he knows I was there. He asked after you. I said you were worn out with the work. That we both were. "Lock work is not an easy job," he said, "being on call day and night to get the barges through." "It's not," I said. You never know, he might leave me something.'

When he walked in through the kitchen door, I had that urge to step off the edge, any edge. I could feel that call to the freedom of nothingness. Is it an inkling of something possible or just a desire to fly? Is this the same unknown that used to make my girlhood dog hesitate, then freeze and gaze into trees at things that didn't appear to me to be there?

Thursday, August 3

It was half past two in the morning when the knock came to the door.

He blundered out of bed.

'If that's a fucking barge running this late, I'll be dug out of the bastards,' he muttered and then he was gone, stumbling down the stairs in the darkness. I heard him unbolting the door in the hallway and there was a voice from outside and his tone changed.

'Come in, Guard,' I heard him say and I was halfway down the narrow stairs before he added: 'Which of them is it?'

The guard turned as I came through the doorway.

'Good night, ma'am,' he said quietly. 'I'm sorry to be disturbing the house in the small hours but we got a call at the barracks from the barracks in Ballitore. About your father.'

'What news?' I asked.

'Not good, ma'am. One of the neighbours was on his way from a card school and saw that the door of your father's house was open. This would be around half twelve or one. He looked in on him to see that all was well, but he found him collapsed, after taking a turn. He sent for the doctor in Moone but there was nothing to be done. They asked that I come with the word as soon as possible. And I'm very sorry to be the bearer of such news.'

Before I could answer, my husband said: 'I thought it was one or other of the childer beyond in London. It's bad news but it's a relief, too.'

I was on my way by three o'clock, cycling through the darkness.

'Not but there's damn all you can do,' my husband said as I wheeled the bike from the shed. 'You'd be better getting a night's sleep.'

I clipped a small case with some clothes onto the carrier, pushed the bike along the track until I got my bearings and then set off cycling through the deepness of the night.

The air was warm. The thought of autumn hadn't yet got even a loose grip on the countryside. The carbide lamp on the bicycle threw enough light for me to make my way and, within half an hour, my eyes had grown accustomed to the darkness and to the outline of the road ahead.

Carlow was sleeping and so was Castledermot, though the dawn was breaking over Fraughan Hill as I freewheeled down into the village, and the sun was rising as I wheeled in the gateway of my father's house just before six o'clock.

Ann Murphy and Mick Byrne stepped into the yard when they heard the bicycle tyres on the gravel and Ann came and hugged me as I left the bike against the wall.

'God love you,' she said, 'and God rest your daddy.'

'Mary Neill was here an hour ago and laid your father out,' Mick said and he extended his hand and shook mine. 'I'm awful sorry for your troubles.'

I looked in his eyes, lit by the rising sun, and saw genuine sorrow, and a second sorrow washed over me. I'd gone to school with Mick and, had I given him the slightest encouragement, he would have asked me to walk out with him, but I didn't. He was too kind, too nice, too soft for me. Yet here he was, being kind and soft and nice, and I respected him for it.

Later, the other neighbours came in dribs and drabs, bringing food and drink, leaving their offerings in the kitchen before coming to sit with me in the bedroom where my father was laid out.

The veins on the backs of his hands ran like deep blue rivers beneath his skin, but his face still held the colour of this summer and another eighty before that and his hair was washed and brushed. I kept waiting for his eyes to open, for a wink to tell me he had fooled us all again, but, instead, his face held the rigid shape of death.

'I seen the door open and I going up to play cards,' Mick told me. 'That would have been about eight o'clock yesterday evening. Your father was standing in the doorway; he was painting the outside of it. "A good evening for it," I said. "'Tis," he said. "God bless the work," I said and then I went on about my business. And I coming back about half twelve, I seen the door still open and something told me to put my head in to see if he was all right. He was sitting there at the table and for a minute I thought he was asleep but when he didn't answer I laid my hand on his and I knew. Straight away. I ran down for Ann and the doctor, and then I went and told the guards in Ballitore. The rest you know.'

Saturday, August 5

I sent a telegram with the funeral arrangements to my husband yesterday and he arrived by hackney just before the funeral Mass this morning. He sat in beside me in the front seat of the church and the neighbours filed in behind us.

Afterwards, he helped carry the coffin the few yards from the church to the open grave where my father was laid beside my mother.

Back at the house, my husband drank too much and talked too much and I was glad when the hackney came to collect him at seven o'clock. He was the worse for wear.

'No rest for some,' he said as he left. 'I'll see you when you get back.'

'In a few days,' I said.

'Hmm.' I could tell he wasn't pleased but then he was gone and I went back inside to talk to my own people. The people I know. The people who know me. The people who were my father's friends all his life and would have been mine had I stayed here.

We talked long into the night. About my father. About my children. About the canal work. About where I lived. But nothing about my husband and no one asked if I was happy. Not because they didn't care but because they didn't want me to have to lie. The sky was lightening before the last of the neighbours left and I dozed, on and off, in a chair by the fire.

Sunday, August 6

I was up and about before cockcrow and I stood in the open doorway of my father's kitchen, a mug of tea in my hand, and surveyed the door he had been painting on the night he died. Half the timbers were a faded cream and half were a fresh, bright blue. The paint tin sat on the floor inside the door. Mick Byrne had put the brush into a jar of turpentine beside it. I smiled and thought about finishing the job my father had started but I didn't.

I'd leave the work half-finished, a reminder to all who passed that James McDermot was dead and a promise to myself that, sometime in the future, I would complete the task he had begun but only when the time was right for me.

I smiled as I heard him say: 'Ne'er a hurry on you, girl. But you'll have to do the whole lot when the time comes or you'll be left with a door that's like a jennet crossed with a zebra.'

After Mass, I stood in the churchyard and chatted with the neighbours. Only when the last one had left did I see Mick Byrne come from the church porch where he had been waiting and watching patiently.

'I have a bit of dinner put on above in the house, to save you cooking,' he said. 'I can drop it down to you or you're more nor welcome to come and join me.'

'You're very thoughtful, Mick. I'll walk up with you if that's all right?'

I hadn't been in his house in more than twenty years and little had changed, yet everything had changed. I still had to duck through the low doorway, into the pantry where the jars were covered by his mother's lacework, the small beads that held the lace covers in place shining in the midday sun.

The kitchen table and chairs were as I remembered but, since his mother's death, Mick had broken out a big window in the back wall, allowing the sunlight to roll across the room.

'Have a seat,' he said and then he set to work, taking a casserole from the oven of the black range that shone in the alcove where I'd often sat as a child.

The best cutlery was brought from a box on the sideboard and the willow pattern plates, which I had never seen his mother use, were taken down from the top shelf of the dresser.

'You've gone to a lot of trouble,' I said.

'Not at all. You've enough to be doing without cooking a dinner.'

We talked about childhood, about his mother and my father and the quiet way they'd both left the world. And then we talked about my mother's death and the Spanish flu and all the people we'd known who had died in 1918 and 1919.

We talked about my children's jobs and about Mick's job as a roadman. But I didn't ask why he had never married and he didn't ask why I had. And, afterwards, he walked me back to my father's house and, before he left, he said: 'If there's anything at all that needs doing, Julie, just say the word.'

'You might keep an eye on the place, Mick,' I said. 'I don't know yet what I'll do with it. You never know, I might even come back and live here.'

I saw him redden a little but he said nothing.

'I'll give you my father's key,' I said, 'if you don't mind looking in now and then.'

'I'd be more than happy to ....'

I thought he was going to say something else but he didn't.

I haven't slept properly in my father's house since Christmas, and tonight I'm finding it hard to sleep. One of the things I miss, now that he's gone, is the heartening sound of his snores. They used to patrol the house, night after night, like a watchman checking every corner of the building that was home. And now there's only the long silence oozing from his empty room, a stillness like a trap unsprung.

Tuesday, August 8

I came back here today. From my home to my house.

At supper time my husband said, 'You'll be thinking of selling the father's place. We could put the money into buying a few acres somewhere. Doing a small bit of farming.'

His life's ambition, but I didn't entertain him.

'Too soon to be doing anything,' I said. 'My father isn't cold in the ground.'

He mumbled something and went on with his meal.

Tuesday, August 15

My husband went to the horse fair in Borris. He who hates horses, who never stops complaining about the barge horses and their dung and their heavy clapping feet on the soft winter banks. But he went and I was pleased to have the place to myself. Pleased to share a few minutes of chat with the bargemen who passed and pleased with the silence that fell back into place once their barges had disappeared around the next slow bend.

This being a Holy Day of Obligation, I took great pleasure in not feeling obliged at all to go to Mass. Instead, I brought woodbine in jars and placed it on the babies' graves in the corner of the field. I rearranged the stones where a passing fox or badger had disturbed them.

In the afternoon I walked up to the woods. The day was overcast and humid and there was an intense quietness, as though the world was waiting for thunder and lightning or rain but they never came.

There is a stream deep in the wood that sings a gentle song at night. I know this because I have often walked up here in the small hours when its notes are a whisper in the dark. The tune it sings then is like the sound of promised light.

Sometimes, when I come up here in October, I hear it as I walk between the trees, like a suggestion of something running hard beneath the hush of autumn dusk, and at its heart I find the tormenting and exciting scent of musk. And that makes me sad because it's a scent I associate with my first months here, a time when I believed happiness would be mine. At first it was the scent of love.

Today I was surprised to find it in the air again. I'd feared it had gone, presumed upon its careless loss. *Not so, not so*, the stream sang.

If my husband ever reads this, he'd have me back inside the gates of The Mental in jig time but he won't. He's still not home, still pretending to size up the horses at Borris fair, even though the clock is striking eleven.

Thursday, August 31

The last day of the month. The end of summer. Early this morning a man passed the house with his dog. He stopped at the lock gates for a smoke. The dog plunged into the dark water and swam about for a while. I watched from the upstairs window as he climbed back out, shook himself and then plunged in again.

Why? I wondered. Why would he do that, dive into the dark coldness of the water on a morning when the air has an edge of autumn to it? And then, as though he'd read my thoughts, the dog climbed out again, shook himself off, looked into the slowly rising mist and seemed to say, *Because I can. Because ....*

I read this back and read the previous entry and notice I have heard streams speak and dogs speak. The madness of my imagination.

Friday, September 1

I love the sound of wind outside my midnight window. It's one of the few good things about autumn and winter. I don't mean a storm but a sharp wind, the kind we used to walk in as children when we had nowhere else to go and nothing else to do. Up the side of Fraughan Hill, arms spread wide, bicycles abandoned on the road below, the gusts nearly lifting us off our feet. Mick Byrne and Annie Corrigan and Birdy Wall and Pat Shaughnessy and me. Five urchins against the elements.

The wind blew all last night and there was a deeper tone to its whistling than you get in summer. I lay awake and thought of my father and mother and of those nights long ago and of someone hurrying a kettle of hot water across a frozen yard, a collar of snow on the pump handle. Pouring the steaming water slowly to release the mechanism, so more water could be pumped for the last pots of tea before the final hand of cards. I thought about leaving houses in the early hours and the way the lane before us would have a trimming of diamonds in the moonlight, and I missed my mother and father and, most of all, I was in despair for the years and the youth that's gone from my life and the way lost time is never to be found again no matter how hard you search.

There I lay, well over halfway through my life and so little to show for it. Nothing to show for it. My children gone, two to England and two into the earth. I'm married to a man I do not love. I live in a house I have no fondness for, on the bank of a river that sometimes, in flood, feels like a threat. I realise full well what might have been and who I might have become and what I might have made of my life.

And then, at dinner time, word came that my husband's uncle had died and by teatime he was on a train heading south, hoping for something from the old man's will, and I was glad to be shut of him for two or three days.

Saturday, September 2

What is it about days that makes them so different? This one began with my waking alone and savouring that aloneness. That was one of the things I had loved in my first few days in The Mental – having a room, a cell, to myself. Having a space to call my own, something I had never had once I married. But then I was moved to a ward where there were twenty other women, and the pleasure of aloneness vanished.

Downstairs, I baked some scones, made tea and sat outside the front door of the house, watching the trees on the small island that separates the lock from the wilder flow of the river beyond. The leaves had begun to shift uneasily, a sure sign that autumn was in the air. We've been blessed with a warm, dry summer and today has the feel of that summer, too, but there won't be many more days like this and so I sat and relished the rinse of sunlight on my skin.

In the early afternoon I walked to the graves and sat there for a while. The sky was a field of unseasonal, heavenly bluebells and, for an hour, I could imagine it was May again; I could imagine I was full-bellied again, carrying one or other of the children to healthy full term. I thought about their faces and who and what they might have been. I pondered names and dreamed them into lives and jobs and loves and children of their own, and I found myself smiling at the thought of these grown children with their own children around their feet.

Only when I had crossed the ditch and picked a handful of damsons from the tree at the end of our garden did I see the chimney of a barge dipping slowly in the lock between the gates. I hurried up the garden and, stepping through the small gate, turned to take the lock key from its box, but it was gone. Moving to the water's edge, I peered down at the grey-haired man who was standing at the tiller of the barge. He was a stranger, not one of the bargemen who plied this route week in, week out.

My shadow fell on the deck and the man looked up and smiled.

'I'm sorry,' I said. 'I was in the field; I didn't know you were here. I'd have opened the lock gates for you.'

'Absolutely no trouble at all,' the man said. 'This is the first time I've been allowed to open gates alone. It's been an adventure.' His accent was English.

'If you need any help ….'

'I'll call out if I do.'

Twenty minutes later, the man knocked quietly on the open kitchen door. 'I've left the key back in the box.'

'Thank you. And, again, apologies. My husband is away at a funeral and I was up the field. We rarely have barges coming through on Saturdays this late in the year.'

'I managed it well enough.'

'Good.'

There was a moment of silence that I felt the need to fill. 'Are you travelling far?'

'Only to the next village. Which is just a few miles downriver, I believe.'

'Yes, just a few miles.'

'I picked up the barge in Athy. I'm contemplating buying it. This is a trial run. For the barge and for me.' He smiled

'Well, you're almost there,' I said.

'I might well tie up here for the evening. If you have no objection?'

'Of course not. You're free to do as you please.' The words sounded dismissive and I blushed. 'I mean, yes, of course, please do.' I blushed again.

The man smiled.

'My name is Paul,' he said and offered his hand.

I had to step forward to take it.

'Julie,' I said.

'I'm very pleased to meet you, Julie.'

There was another silence and, again, I felt the need to fill it. 'I've just picked some damsons. You might like to try them.'

'That would be very nice.'

I put the damsons in a bowl and handed it to him. He thanked me and went back to his barge.

Darkness had just fallen when I heard a knock on the still-open front door. It was the Englishman again.

'Have you eaten?' he asked.

'Not since the middle of the day.'

'I'm just cooking some food if you'd care to join me? I have more than enough for two.'

I hesitated.

'Don't feel you have to. I just thought ....'

'Thank you,' I said. 'I'd be happy to.'

'The food will be ready in fifteen minutes.' And then he was gone.

I went upstairs and changed into my best dress. Why did I do that? Because it was an occasion. Because I hadn't eaten a full meal anywhere in years other than my own kitchen, the refectory in The Mental or my father's kitchen, with the exception of the Sunday when Mick Byrne cooked for me. Because I was pleased to be asked.

The Englishman was waiting on the deck and extended his hand to help me on board. I followed him down into the galley where he had set the small table. A jam jar, filled with the last of the summer's wildflowers, sat on the table. I offered him some of the scones I had baked earlier. He thanked me and indicated a seat at the head of the table.

'It'll be basic food,' he said. 'A lifetime of cooking for myself.'

'A lifetime of cooking for others,' I said. 'So being cooked for is a great treat.'

We sat and ate and talked. In the beginning he did most of the talking. His name is Paul Abbott. He had come to Ireland to look at barges. He thinks it might be cheaper to buy one here and have it shipped to England. He lives in Leamington Spa. He is contemplating living on a barge on the Grand Union Canal.

'The first wild thing I've done in my life,' he said.

'I don't believe I've ever done anything wild,' I said. 'Apart from marrying my husband because of the brightness of his waistcoat and that turned out to be a mistake.'

'I'm sorry to hear that,' Paul said quietly. 'How long have you been married?'

'Twenty-two years. Chances are we're more than halfway to the finishing line.'

'Thinking like that seems a waste of life.'

'Does it?'

'Well, there must be pleasures in your life. Enjoyments.'

'Books,' I said.

'Well, bless you and your fellow readers. I run a bookshop in Leamington. The Quiet Corner. Without you readers, I'd be out walking the roads with a pack on my back.'

I told him about the dictionary my father gave me. I told him about the books I'd read in the previous year. I told him about my father's death and then I told him about the children buried in the field above the house.

'Would it be an impertinence if I were to ask you to take me to their burial place?' he said. 'It may not be something you wish to do, certainly not at this hour of the night.'

'I often go up there at night. I'd very much like you to see where they are.'

He took two jackets from a hook behind him and offered me one.

'It's probably a little chilly outside,' he said.

I slid my hands into the sleeves and pulled the jacket round my shoulders. It felt snug, warm with the comfort of being well-worn. I drew it tight about me.

Outside, the waning gibbous moon threw shadows from the apple and the damson trees. I led the way through a small gap in the hedge and out into the pale, damp field. We walked in silence, side by side, to the graves in the corner where the black-berried hedges meet. The white stones were ashen in the half-light. I told him the names I had given the lost children, names I had read in a book long ago. Strange, beautiful names.

We stood for a long time as the spectre of the moon climbed silently through the sky and the flicker of its light slowly pulled the shade of the hedges back to nothingness. I could feel the wetness of the grass through my shoes and the mist of the night-time on my hair.

'You probably want to get back to your barge,' I said at last but Paul didn't answer.

After a long time, he said, 'Thank you for bringing me here. I am privileged.'

We walked back the way we'd come, still in silence. Only when we reached the riverbank did he speak. 'I know it's late but would you care to join me for a cup of tea or coffee before you retire?'

'I would,' I said. I didn't want these special hours to end. I didn't want our conversation and our silences to be gone.

In the galley, Paul threw some kindling into the stove and built a fire that sent heat through the small space in no time. He toasted two scones on forks before the fire and spread them with butter that melted into the dough. We sat at the small table and ate and drank and talked.

'I love the word communion,' I said. 'I don't mean in the way priests and religions use it. I mean in the true sense. This is a communion.'

'What is the true sense to you?'

'The sharing of thoughts and feelings on a personal or, maybe, a mystical level. Sorry, I'm sounding mad.'

'You're not.'

And then I told him about my time in The Mental.

'Why were you there?' His tone was neither critical nor negative. His question was simply a question.

'My husband asked the doctor to put me there.'

'But why?'

'He said I was *acting quare*. His words, not mine.'

'Meaning?'

'Meaning he saw me on two nights leave the house and go down to the river and stand there naked because my body was burning. Meaning one day I cycled the miles to Bagenalstown and got on a train and I had no idea where I was going or why. I just needed to go.'

'But that's not madness!'

'The doctor said it was the change, that I might be better in care for a while. My husband said I was soft in the head, that I was liable to make a show of myself and him at any time. That I was a danger to myself and others.'

'And are you?' Paul asked but he was smiling.

'Do you feel you're in danger?' I asked.

By way of answer, he covered my hand with his.

It was well past one in the morning when Paul walked me to my door.

'I've so enjoyed talking to you,' he said. 'I hope we can talk again when I'm on my way back up river.'

'That depends on when.'

'Tuesday or Wednesday. I plan to do some walking when I get to the next village downstream. To be honest, walking is a greater part of my life than boating.'

'My husband will be home on Monday, from the funeral. It's unlikely we'll have much chance to talk. He'll be here. He wouldn't like the idea of our talking.'

'I understand. Well, for tonight, thank you. For taking me to see where your children are lying, thank you.

For trusting me with your story, thank you. And, most of all, for your company.'

He kissed my hand and then was gone into the darkness between the house and the water. I stood in the kitchen that seemed, suddenly, different – smaller, filled with a half-imagined promise and with a fear that this short benediction in my life would simply fade away like the moon in the light of morning.

Sunday, September 3

The sun this blessèd morning rose just after half past six but I had already been up and about for an hour. A dozen times I went upstairs to peep through the curtains at the barge moored just below the lock, to reassure myself that it was still there.

I baked a loaf of brown soda bread and, while it cooled on the kitchen table, I opened the front door. A moment later there was a gentle tap and Paul was standing in the doorway.

'I thought,' he said, 'before I journeyed onward that I might check with you regarding your plans for today?'

'I have no plans,' I said.

'Well then, I wondered whether we might travel the few miles to the next village and return here this evening.'

'You wanted to spend a few days walking there.'

'I can walk elsewhere, tie up and walk elsewhere in the coming days. I thought you might like to travel downriver today. I assure you, we'll be back before nightfall.'

'I'd like that very much.'

In all my years as a lock-keeper's wife, I had never travelled more than a hundred yards on a barge. The bargemen had, once or twice, asked if I'd like to be on board as the boats descended or ascended through the lock system, but, apart from those brief trips, I had never voyaged beyond the end of the walkway.

Today was a new adventure. We left the lock and the house behind and Paul edged the barge out into the water. I watched my home fade in the early morning mist and felt no sense of regret, only one of possibility and, dare I say it, excitement.

The bank, which I have walked a thousand times over the years, took on a new appearance as we moved slowly downstream. I watched the waterhens come and go from their nests beneath the overhang; the swans glided by us in pairs, and as we approached the next lock, a solitary swan drifted by, his eyes set firmly on us.

'It's as though he's jealous of our companionship.' I surprised myself with the sound of my own voice and the words I had spoken.

'"True friendship can afford true knowledge,"' Paul said.

I smiled.

'Thoreau,' he said. 'Do you know his work?'

I shook my head.

'You must read him. His book *Walden*. "I had three chairs in my house; one for solitude, two for friendship, three for society." I've often wished I could have followed his philosophy. "Beware of all enterprises that require new clothes." Now, that is solid advice.'

Paul talked about Thoreau and Walden Pond and Thoreau's time living there. I listened, drinking in the story that seemed so apt for our quiet journey down an almost deserted river.

Paul opened the lock gates and slowly we ascended until the barge was in line with the second set of gates. I listened to the water fill about us, a sound I'd heard hundreds of times yet never really heard at all.

'You should live on this barge,' I said as we moved back out onto the wider water of the river.

'Do you think?'

'It's bigger than Thoreau's cabin, from what you tell me.'

'It is.'

'And it has just two chairs and one form.'

'True.'

At the village bridge we tied up and walked along the bank for a mile or two. I told Paul about my children and their work in London.

'Have you been to see them?' he asked.

'No. If I went, I'd likely never come back.'

'Is that a good reason for not going?'

'No, I suppose not. But – and this may sound strange – I feel they're doing well. They seem happy, they're making new lives, I'm not sure I could leave the two babies here. Does that make me sound as if I should be back in the psychiatric hospital?'

Paul shook his head. We walked on in silence and then, as we turned to walk back the way we'd come, he said: 'There are other choices, Julie. You could visit your son and daughter, knowing you would come back. Or you could take the … spirit … no, that's not the correct word … the energy of your two babies, take it in your heart and carry it with you. That strength and sense of their personalities is more than just memory. It's something substantial. Does that make sense?'

'Yes,' I said.

'Think on it. You're a young, beautiful woman with ideas and imagination. Don't let where you are and who you're with extinguish that energy.'

'I'm forty-four,' I said.

'Exactly. Forty-four, not sixty-four, not eighty-four.'

'I've already outlived my mother by five years.'

'And you told me your father was eighty when he died. Live in the light of his life, live your life. I don't mean to sound callous but you cannot live the lives of the dead; you can only live your own life. Live it!'

In mid-afternoon, as we journeyed back, Paul cut the engine and tied up at the deserted bank of a long field that swept up from the river to the empty sky above it. He carried a basket from the galley and then the small table and the two chairs and laid out a picnic on the deck. We sat in the warm sun, the last of the season's wasps buzzing about us, and ate and drank, mostly in silence.

Afterwards, I helped him carry the chairs down to the galley. As I turned to climb the few steps up to the deck, he asked if he might kiss me. I didn't hesitate but took his weather-beaten face in my hands, touched the ends of his wild grey hair and kissed him on the mouth. And then his tongue was in my mouth and his hands were in my hair and it was impossible to tell where my body began and his ended, so close were we in those moments. I never wanted that time to end. I never wanted not to be with him. I had no regret, no sense of wrongness or what the priests like to call sin. I had nothing but the need and the want to be held and kissed.

That night, as the sun set just after eight, I carried a basket of bread from the house to the barge and we sat, well wrapped against the autumn chill, and we talked and the moon rose through a still, hollow sky and the crows fell silent and no one came and no one went along the misty bank. And, after we had said all we had to say, we lay together on a rug on the barge deck and we made love. His hands lifted my dress above my head and his tongue swept over my tiny breasts like a warm, soft wave. Down it travelled, moving between my ribs, across my belly and between my thighs. No one had ever kissed me there. His lips touched my wetness, his tongue slid inside me, waking a sensation I had never dreamed, much less experienced. His face was buried between my legs and my breath became a long, deep cry and I didn't care who heard or saw.

We slept on the deck, wrapped in a rug, folded in each other, but I woke to the desperation of parting.

Just before the barge pulled away, Paul handed me a book.

'I think you'll enjoy it,' he said. 'My card is inside. Use it as a bookmarker and then, when you come to see your children, you can visit me in Leamington. You can spend some time on the barge or in my house. As long as you wish.'

In the late afternoon, my husband returned. He had been drinking. 'Well,' was all he said and then he went upstairs and fell asleep on our bed.

Tuesday, September 5

I have spent two days thinking about the *if only* but, of course, there is nothing to be gained from that. I have no sense of regret about what happened, only sadness about the *if only*.

I have begun to read the book Paul gave me: *Of Mice and Men* by John Steinbeck. Even taking it from its place on the shelf brings a tingle of excitement. This is a book that Paul has read and when I turn a page I know he has turned the same page.

It crossed my mind this afternoon to take my bike and cycle along the towpath in the hope of catching up with his boat, but what purpose would that serve? I spent an hour imagining the hubbub that would result if I went with him and left my bike on the riverbank. The searching that would follow. The assumption that my body had been washed down the river. And all the while I'd be on my way to England with Paul. But I won't do that, I know. And Paul might not want me to. If our night on the barge is a memory, the thought of fleeing from here is simply a daydream.

I have written Paul's address into one of my notebooks. A line here, a line there, a telephone number – scattered so that they can't easily be found or put together. And his card is hidden at the back of a chest of drawers in the bedroom. Already, I've taken it out and touched and read and reread it half a dozen times.

If only, if only, if only, if only, if only, if only, if only, if only if only if only if only

Thursday, September 14

This morning I stood in the little orchard where the apples are almost ready for picking and the plums are weighted with the heaviness of the summer gone and I listened for dreams of the past but I couldn't be certain about what was real or what was imagined or if a memory becomes something imagined, like a dream, at some point in our lives, when it is beyond recovery, and survives only in the remembering.

Do dreams die with the dreamers who dreamed them? Are my father's dreams and my mother's dreams disappeared with them or do they go on in time, in that vast, uncertain place where we travel when we hope and aspire to other things? Could someone's hopes be there among the trees, colliding with mine? If I reach to pick an apple from one of those trees, am I, in some strange way, reaching across the years and sensing something of the man or woman who picked an apple from the same tree forty years ago, some woman who lived in this house and slept in the room where I now sleep? How do I know what is *now* or what is an inkling of the past? If I see a shadow here at twilight, as I climb through the hedge on my way to visit the babies, am I seeing a shadow or the ghost of someone who lived and worked here a hundred years ago? Who sowed these trees as saplings, who gathered the first fruit? Are their memories and dreams still here, sadly colliding with mine?

So many questions to ponder and only one answer: I do not know. All I can do is stand in the evening light and imagine the ghosts as they come and go.

Monday, September 25

Forget-me-nots are still blooming on a late September bank as though to say *forget me not*.

In the Lilac Field I saw a wake of crows grazing the stubble and a handful of brighter pigeons among them. The lilac is long gone but I picked the last woodbine of summer from the hedge, took it home and placed it in a jam pot on the window. The last wild rose of summer.

And this evening, as I stepped onto the lane to collect the milk can from the branch where young Dorgan leaves it, a shower of sparrows lifted from the hedge and settled on a beech in the opposite hedge. Who needs angels or the thought of them?

Saturday, September 30

As we sat at our kitchen table, the night already drawn in, my husband said: 'D'you know, the chances are that someone who lives in one of the houses between here and the town will find me dead on the road some Sunday. I'm well aware of that and of what I've become. I'm not the man you married. I'm a disappointment to you and myself.'

Oh, but you are, I thought, you are that man. And I tried hard to feel a pity but there's little pity or care left in me for my husband any longer.

Monday, October 2

This morning, as I was cycling to town, I saw, on the side of a hill, beneath a great tree, young boys, stone gatherers, strung out across the slope, looking in their bent selves like boulders. An east wind was blowing up the field and, even in passing, I could sense the coldness all around them. Now and then, one boy would stand and stretch and the bitterness of the day seemed to be in the slowness of his movement.

On the headland, the farmer stood with his dog, watching the boys fanned out across the land, gathering the stones into sacks, hefting the heavy jute over their shoulders and carrying the loads to a place in the top corner of the field where a small mountain of gathered rocks was growing against the mist of the morning sky. Had these boys been there since first light or was the small mountain the result of the previous day's labour?

In town, I did the shopping I needed, bought a book in the bookshop and drank a cup of tea in the café on the corner, leafing through the book as I did. It's called *Man's Search for Meaning* by Viktor Frankl.

Something about those first few pages got me thinking about my own life. It has been lived in relative ease. I was loved at my first home. I had a job I liked. I had many friends in Waterford. I married a man I thought I loved. I lost two children but I have two children who love me and whom I love dearly. I am not hungry. I am not often angry. Sometimes I am very sad. Mostly I am simply a little sad. This is how I can best describe who and what I am:

My life is like a jumper that cannot be unravelled. The holes will always be there, snagged on nails and the rough edges of door frames or caught in bending under haw branches.

Sometimes I feel I am working as hard as a bird in winter to be the person people expect me to be and to behave in the way people expect a grown woman to behave.

Strange things give me pleasure. I love fields that have no gates, their drills and stubbled crops thrown open to the passing world. I love fields that say, *Come in, be a part of us, be with us, be in us, taste our sorrel, pick fruit from our ditches, dig crops from our soil, lie in our grass, smell the honeysuckle that twines through our trees.*

Cycling home, the same boys, still picking stones, had moved up the hill. The rocky mountain had grown wider and higher. The farmer and his dog were seated, the farmer on a five-barred gate, the dog at his feet.

Friday, October 6

The summer has got a second wind with a late flowering of flies. This morning, when I was doing the washing in the tin bath, I couldn't keep them out of the kitchen, their rattling buzz and humming against the window panes was like a grinding but not inside my head. The noise was out there somewhere, in a corner of the room, inside and out. The slimmest slice of sunlight brought them swarming, their summer bodies swollen like long-dead calves that pass in the spring river before being washed up on the mucky banks.

Monday, October 9

Today a parcel came with an English stamp.

'That'll be from Margaret or Robert,' the postman said as he stood in the kitchen doorway, sheltering from a shower.

'It will,' I said, though I knew the writing was neither my son's nor my daughter's.

'That rain is down for a while,' the postman said.

But I knew what he was really saying.

'You'll have a cup of tea?' I asked.

'If you're having one yourself.'

I pulled the kettle onto the range.

'Himself is not at home?'

'No. He's taking dead wood from the weir. It came down in the flood we had the other night.'

'That'll dry nicely for next winter.'

I poured his tea, then slipped the parcel into the press, behind the jars of jam.

'The pair are doing well beyont in England?'

'They are.'

'Better there nor here.'

Only when my husband had gone to bed, and I could hear his occasional snore through the bedroom floor, did I take the parcel from the press and slowly open it. Paul had obviously taken note of the name on the lock gates and addressed the letter to me at The Lock House.

Inside was a book, *Walden* by Henry David Thoreau, and inside the front flap of the book was an envelope holding two sheets of paper and a photograph of the interior of his bookshop, rows of shelves, an armchair here and there, a small counter.

His letter was written in a neat hand, far neater than my own. I put it aside and opened the second sheet. It contained a short poem:

My evening lamp is fading fast,
its burning ember will not last,
but what's to come and what is past,
in this moment, all are one.

I read it a number of times and then returned to the letter, hoping it would provide some information on the verse.

4th October 1950

Dear Julie,

I hope my memory of the name of the lock at which you live is correct. Otherwise this letter and Mr Thoreau will disappear into the wide blue somewhere.

I had intended writing earlier but, between one thing and another, that didn't happen. There are a few drafts of this in my wastepaper basket – attempts that were abandoned.

The trip back to Athy on the barge was unremarkable, apart from the fact that I missed your company. I didn't spend a few days walking. Instead, I returned to Leamington ahead of schedule.

I have thought so much about our meeting and about our conversations and I hope they are as important to you as they are to me. What I would give to be sitting on the deck again, chatting and solving the world's problems. Though, in these damp October days, the likelihood of sitting in the open air is not great. Most of all, I hope we get to meet again. You really should consider travelling to see your children in London. (My reasons for saying this are somewhat selfish, I admit.) The London train comes right to Old Warwick Road – an interesting walk from my shop. Or I could travel to London if that better suited.

Failing that, I might well take another barge trip along the Barrow waters in the coming year. But next summer seems a lifetime away.

I hope you are well and I hope you will consider what I said to you about carrying the energy of the babies within you. You will not be leaving them, just as they have never left you.

If you find time, please do write. It is rare to find someone who is so open, and so easy to be open with, as you.

Paul

P.S. I enclose a short verse I wrote on the trip back to Athy. I thought about my life and about what it has been and what it might be and how everything coalesced in those moments together. Wordsworth it is not!

I read the letter and the poem again and sat for a long time composing in my mind a reply to Paul's words. Had I expected to hear from him? In the days after his going, I thought there might be a card or letter but, as the weeks passed, I tried to put him out of mind. Not because I wanted to but because there seemed little point in hoping against hope. And now here was this letter, inviting me to visit. Offering to meet me in London. I found myself pleased at the offer but uncertain that I would ever find the energy to leave here and travel in the knowledge that I might never return.

Once in my life I did something unplanned, fell for someone on a whim, chased a gaudy waistcoat. Am I likely to do the same thing again, go running in pursuit of a barge with its cramped living quarters and a man about whom I know very little?

A business card, a few conversations, a letter and a poem do not necessarily make for a lifetime – or half a lifetime – of happiness. Even lovemaking does not guarantee love. Yet I was flattered and pleased, but I knew this was no time to make a decision; no time, even, to reply.

Tuesday, October 10

While my husband was out dealing with a barge, I reread Paul's letter. Then I hid it and the poem with the book he gave me. They are safe behind the panelling of a wardrobe in Margaret's room.

I went walking along the bank, following the course we took that Sunday afternoon on the barge. How different the world looks. The leaves falling, a mist sitting on the land, the river disappearing into the uncertain light of five o'clock.

On my way back I thought about the last year. This time twelve months ago I was probably walking this same path. I hadn't yet been committed. That word. It sounds like a sin. We commit sins, venial and mortal. My sin on the boat, five weeks ago, would turn the parish priest's face to a red jelly if I told him. Needless to say, I won't.

When did I last step inside a confession box? The week before I married, twenty-two years ago. And I listened while a middle-aged man gave me advice on marriage and on what would satisfy my husband and what should be my satisfaction. And he was right. It was about my husband's satisfaction and rarely mine. I was supposed to be happy with the outcome, with pregnancy and children, or no children. The rest was *in the hands of God*. But the dead children were not in the hands of God; they were in Limbo. The parish priest sat at my kitchen table and explained, very slowly, as though I was a stupid woman, that Limbo was 'the temporary place set aside for the souls of the just who are excluded from the vision of God until Christ's ascension into heaven. And that includes unbaptized children and others who die without grievous personal sin but are excluded from the vision of God on account of their original sin.' And then he sat back and drank from his teacup and slipped a slice of cake into his mouth and waited for me to nod or agree but I just went on staring at him, sure that I wanted no part of his religion if this was the best it had to offer.

If I had spoken my mind then, I might have been committed too. *Depressed by the loss of the child, post-natal depression*, the report would read.

And I think about the year and how that year and any year is the accumulation of a lifetime. Things rarely happen out of the blue.

Making love to Paul was not something that came out of the blue. If it had been, I might regret it now, feel guilty for myself and sad for my husband, but I don't. I feel no guilt. I feel only gratitude for what Paul did and gladness for what I did.

And nor was my making love to Paul some kind of reaction against a Church that has no room to even bury children such as mine, or the priest who told me not to worry, I could have another child, or the husband who had me locked up because I walked beside a river in the small hours to cool myself, to stand and look at the world from a different place, just to be there because I wished to be there.

None of their dogma is of any interest to me. None of my husband's petty ideas matter. I try to live my own life in my own way. And yet I cannot say I truly do. I live where it is safe to live. I live in a pretended closeness to my husband. I walk in the autumn sunshine, though, often, I am in love with the thought of Mr Frost.

And I feel a deep, dark sadness at Paul's absence now from my life. A regret that I cannot see him, touch him, meet him, talk and listen to him. Be close to his body. The ache is in my stomach. This morning it was in my head and tonight it will be between my thighs.

Friday, October 13

I have two cottages which I visit every year. Two deserted buildings. One appears in autumn and one appears in spring.

The autumn one is a cottage not too far from here, a stone cottage from God knows when. It has been deserted for as long as I can remember, certainly since before my time in these parts. In late spring and summer it disappears beneath a blind of growth. The only thing that alerts the passer-by to its presence in summer is the rambling rose that rises through the alder and elder that have sprung up over the decades. Otherwise, there is a wall of greenery and branches between the road and the cottage which remove it from view. The low wall that once fronted the garden has crumbled beneath the nudges and shoulders of bushes that have grown into trees over the years.

But, in autumn, the cottage reappears from beneath its summer growth; the empty windows all stoop low and hunch to take the weight of winter on their lintels and I make my pilgrimage to walk through its three deserted rooms. I stand in the open fireplace that is taller than me and listen to the scratchy cawing of the crows in the old chimney that is stuffed now with nests and the dereliction of nests. I bend beneath the lintel that takes me into what must once have been a bedroom. The small openings that were windows, back and front, are latticed with branches, laced with ivy. The little light from my carbide lamp falls on a clay floor and walls that were whitewashed faithfully for years but have lost all colour now.

And back I go, across the kitchen floor, into the other bedroom. There, too, the window panes have returned to sand. One wooden frame remains, a dash of red paint flaking slowly into the rotting timber. A name is scratched onto the sill. *Patrick Clowry*. Someone who lived here or someone, like myself, passing through the empty rooms? I have no idea.

On my way back to the house, I bring apples to the workhorse in the Long Field.

Tuesday, October 17

This morning I cycled to town. Before I left, my husband said: 'You don't usually go to the town of a Tuesday.'

'I have library books to return,' I lied.

He sighed that sigh that lets me know exactly what he thinks of books and libraries.

'Bring me back twenty Woodbine,' he said.

'All right.'

I pushed the bike out through the garden gateway.

'And a box of matches,' he called from the doorway.

'All right,' I said over my shoulder.

He went back inside and I cycled away, my letter to Paul in the basket of the bike.

This is what I wrote.

Dear Paul,

By the time you'd gone back home, the swallows had dipped the wires one last time, taking wing for Africa. I remembered you, all smiles, waving from the stern of the barge, your hand on the tiller.

Returned, returned to Leamington.

Will either one of us return when the swallows do?

Julie

Thursday, October 19

Last night there was a strong wind and this morning the road at the bend was littered with fallen chestnuts, mostly still in their shells.

When Margaret and Robert were small, we had a ritual in mid-October. We called it *going to the sea.*

We'd pack a picnic, get dressed for the weather and walk the avenue beneath the falling beech leaves to the bend where the chestnut tree arches out across the roadway. There we'd sit on the roadside, on the huge roots of the chestnut, and have our picnic. And then we'd gather the chestnut cases and tap them with stones till they opened, revealing their shining fruit.

My father had told me as a child that chestnuts were inland pearls. 'Their shine, when you open them fresh, are like the shine of pearls, only better,' he'd say.

And I passed that story to my children as we sat and marvelled at the shine and shape of the season's freshest fall.

This morning I sat on the same roots and opened the husks and watched the chestnuts shine in the low October sun.

Sunday, October 22

Still autumn comes on, digging in now, the days shortening, the way a runner's knees constrict and brace in rushing down a hill, tensed tight against the weight and speed of the summer left behind. But for today, it's levelled out, the quietness disturbed only by the abrupt falling of a leaf.

A bright kingfisher, rich feathers lit by summer gone, darts down the river that is lush with fallen leaves, intent only upon the breath in which it flies. It has no thought of the season past, no thought of Christmas yet to come. October bird, its flight is the only movement in this immobile day.

Thursday, October 26

I am sitting in the kitchen. There is still warmth from the range. Outside the wind and rain hammer on the windows and the doors but in here, if someone was to look at me, they'd see a woman sitting quietly with a book and a journal at her table. They'd see tranquillity. They'd see a living lie.

There must have been a time, other than the first few months, when I loved my husband, when we were happy. There must be things, beyond the graves he made for our children, that I can remember and be joyful about, gifts of his that made my life with him that much richer. Can it be that I have blocked them out, that there are many days and times and things that would speak of his goodness and that I have forgotten them all?

Here is the warm wooden kitchen table where we sat in evening light and ate our supper. *Nobody*. That word was thrown haphazardly, as though our future was his to decide. And now he has thumped up the stairs and climbed into bed and I'm left with this darkness, this night, and the heart begins to shrivel. My heart retreats in fear. There are shadows, there is dread. A fear that I will never be anything but the lock-keeper's wife. That life will have been a patch of sunlight glimpsed in passing the gate of a field. Nothing more.

The crows have gathered on the winter trees; the final swallow has long fled. This evening's words of criticism came from his mouth rehearsed and, later, the gabbled platitude. But the bitterness remains, like another figure sitting across the table from me. The flakes of bogus gratitude have flittered away on the wind outside.

As ever, it began with criticism of the children, of their leaving, of their not sending money, of their not being grateful. And then it moved to me, how I have turned them against him, driven them away, made the house a place *nobody* wants to be. And then there came the silence, followed by the explanation. He doesn't really mean what he says. He had hoped to inherit a small bit of land in his uncle's will; he had dreams of our moving away from here, of leaving water and locks and barges behind. Of making a life on a small farm. Of starting again. Of not becoming the man his father was, a broken-backed lock-keeper with gnarled fingers and a body destroyed by the seasons and the work.

I tried to hear what he was saying. I tried to sympathise. I tried to acknowledge that life might be better, for him at least, away from here. I told him I was sorry his uncle had written him out of the will but there was nothing in my heart that could get beyond the mouthing of words.

'Will you ever think of sellin', your father's place?' he asked.

'Maybe,' I said, 'but just not yet. I'm not ready to let it go.'

He nodded.

'Will you come upstairs with me?' he asked, like a little boy afraid of the dark.

'I'll be up in a while,' I said because I couldn't face the thought of his body on mine, his hands all over me, his seed spilling into me or onto me.

And he knew my postponement was a rejection and he left without a word. No longer the small boy but, instead, the angry man.

No doubt there are shadows in his life, too. No doubt there is dread. Shapes gather on the winter trees; the summer rose is truly dead and gone. Life for each of us is a darkness, a storm beyond our control. Whatever was there has wasted away; our tiny, squalid souls rehearse their flight.

Sunday, October 29

I've been thinking about the word *cunt.*

I found it once in a book by D.H. Lawrence and the writer made it sound beautiful and delicate and sensual. It became a word with a different sound and a different meaning on the page. I try to imagine how it would sound in Paul's mouth, but I can't.

Sometimes my husband uses the word when bargemen upset him, when he thinks they don't value his work – *stupid cunts*, he'll say. It's probably part of what gets under his skin, not being valued. And I'm guilty in that regard. I don't value or love or care about him any more. Nor have I for a long, long time.

And sometimes, after he's had a few and then another few, he'll call me a stupid cunt.

I grew to hate the word and now I think I would like to grow to like it or, at least, to hear it as different word, carrying a softer, kinder meaning. And that change of heart, if it comes, will be down to one book and one Englishman whose barge edged through the lock outside my door on that charmed September day that seems so long ago.

Wednesday, November 1

Yesterday I cycled back to my father's house, to my home place, to my home. Where I live is not my home. I may have had four children in the lock house and raised two of them and baked and washed and cleaned and cooked and gardened and painted and read nearly two thousand books but there were only short periods when I thought of the lock house as my home.

When we first married I thought I might be happy inside those walls, though the constant fall of water over the lock gates and the constant smell of water in the air was never to my liking. In spring and summer and early autumn they were bearable but in winter the sound and scent of water lay, and still lies, like a sickness in the place.

And then there were the bodies whose final living and dying journeys ended at the lock gates. One, of the many, I will never forget. I still have dreams and nightmares about it.

It was a very early morning in July of 1943. I woke to the sound of the deep, gloomy bark of a dog outside the house. Anxious not to wake the children, I poked and pulled at my husband until he, too, was awake.

'It's just a stray,' he said. 'It'll go about its business. If you go out to it, you'll never be shut of it.' And, with that, he was asleep again.

The barking went on, a growl, a bark, a growl and then a splash as the animal jumped into the canal basin. And then silence. I pulled on my dressing gown and hurried downstairs. As I opened the front door, the light was fragile but strong enough to see the animal claw its way back onto the bank where the island divides canal from river. The barking started again, the frantic dog racing up and down along the bank, its eyes fixed on the water.

I walked down the garden path and the sound of the low gate opening caught the dog's attention. Our eyes met and then it plunged back into the water, diving and resurfacing and then diving, again, into the deep water that still held fast to night. But this time the dog did not surface. I knelt above the lock basin, my knees on the cold granite blocks of the wall, and called, whistled, willing the animal to reappear but there was nothing, no sound, no disturbance of the water. Nothing.

Had I dreamt all this? Was I hallucinating? Had I left the dog in the land of nightmares and woken to an imagined memory? I peered into the dark murk of the lock water but, even on a summer day, that water will hold its own secrets and refuse to share them. And then, as I was about to leave, the dog surfaced, soaked and dead, his black coat shining, halfway between the island and the spot where I knelt. And, almost immediately, the body of what appeared to be a man, dressed in trousers and a shirt, surfaced six feet from the dead animal. Both corpses rested on the face of the water. The rising sun sent a shaft of early lemon light, washing them in a delicate glow, and it seemed to me that every bird stopped singing for that moment.

Afterwards, my husband and two guards and the ambulance driver dragged man and dog ashore. They wrapped the man's body in a tarpaulin and carried it to the ambulance. The dog's carcass was tossed into the running stream of the river on the other side of the island.

That is the lock house. But here, in my father's house: no sound of water, no scent of dampness, no bodies making their way into the trap of the wooden gates. Here is the soft chuckling of the pigeons in the trees and the light wind that crosses the valley from Mullaghcreelan Hill. I could live here. This was my home and could be again. What would I be leaving? A house I dislike, a man I despise.

But I'd be leaving, too, the bodies of my babies. Their ghosts, the only sign they'd ever breathed or been inside me.

I sat in the kitchen and made some tea. All the house windows were open onto a still, cold day. I had lit some sticks in the range to discourage the rooks from building. I thought of a day when my father's father was visiting. He sat at the kitchen table and spoke of Black 47. I was a little girl, no more than seven or eight. He was telling stories to my parents of his life as a young man in a famine-scourged country.

'Men and women lay down against the hides of dying calves and shed their tears against the skin and bone or what was left of them.'

'Why didn't they eat the calves?' I asked.

My grandfather sighed and said: 'You're too young to know, Julie girl, too young to know.'

I didn't question any further. There was something in my grandfather's sigh, some deep, dark resignation that said *Enough, enough, don't ask.*

And he never spoke to me of it again. I never heard the stories he had kept in his memory – in the hope, no doubt, of their being passed to the next generation. My generation.

My grandfather was right; I was too young. Instead, I went about the business of delight, ran out through the open door, across the yard and into the turf shed with its smell of summer heat, past the pigsty with its smiling snuffle of a sow, and played with my doll in the darkened quietness beneath the rhubarb leaves.

That other world was there for me; I know that now when it's too late. If only I had known.

Sunday, November 5

I am back at the lock house. I left Moone in the late morning and took my time along the way. Stopped off in Castledermot and bought myself a quarter pound of biscuits in McEvoy's shop. Some I ate as I cycled; the rest I saved to have for my supper. I stopped, again, in Carlow and bought a newspaper.

The house is empty. Too early yet for my husband's return. He'll come rolling home in a couple of hours with some sarcastic comment on his tongue but I'll ride out the storm. He'll slobber through his dinner, then disappear to bed and leave me to my evening of peace.

I'll make some tea, arrange my biscuits on a plate, sit and read. And then I'll write to both Margaret and Robert in London, giving them a version of my life that tells only of the happenings and nothing of the loneliness and disappointment. Children have no need to know these things. I never heard my father once complain after my mother died, and yet his heart must have been crushed. Their happiness was obvious to all.

I consider writing to Paul. What would I say? *I think about you every day. You are my last thought at night. I never walk the bank of the river without seeing you on your barge, without hearing your voice, without telling you how important you are to me.*

After my husband had staggered up to bed, I spread the newspaper on the kitchen table, made some tea, set the biscuits on a plate and read the news. A plane crash on Mont Blanc in France has killed everyone on board; George Bernard Shaw has died aged ninety-four; the Pope says God took the Blessed Virgin's body to heaven after her death. But not the bodies or even the souls of my babies.

I thought about the workhorse in the Long Field, about his solitary life. Does he miss the work and the companionship of people, or is he content to sleep in the long quiet night, standing beneath the chestnut?

Monday, November 6

A morning when the light is so clear I can almost reach across the river, nearly touch the hills as they lean down to meet me.

Every house on the Ridge is sharply defined in the low and brittle light, doors pitched open to this day borrowed from the summer, a low heat at noon that would pass for the heat of sunrise in the heart of June.

I thought about a woman I met in The Mental, a beautiful, gentle woman called Margaret Walsh. She was from somewhere up in the north of Kildare and she'd been locked up for much the same reasons as myself. And, like me, she lived on the banks of a canal and they put her away because she took to wandering the banks in the night and slipping into the water to cool the fever inside her.

We walked the garden together a couple of times, chatting. I wonder whether she's back home again?

Tuesday, November 7

The weather continued fine today, a strange heat from the midday sun. I walked up to the Little Wood beyond the hill, no more than an acre of trees, but at the heart of the sycamores and ash trees are half a dozen oak trees.

These oaks are evergreen and so, in winter, they become my singing trees, reminding me that the dark season will pass and the light will come again.

And beneath the midday sun, shining in a clear sky, with no hint of wind from north or east, I took off my clothes in the shadow of the oaks and closed my eyes and dreamed myself a summer. Enough to have me locked up again.

Friday, November 10

Two letters came today from England, one from Margaret and one from Paul. I read Margaret's and left it on the kitchen table for my husband to see when he came in. The other I kept in my apron pocket until he had gone to bed. There it sat all day, like something warm against my hip, like the warmth of Paul's kisses against my thighs on that September night.

After our supper my husband and I listened to the Home Service on the radio. *Report to the People* was about juvenile delinquents in London.

'And that's where you're happy to have your son and daughter,' he said.

'They're not delinquents,' I told him.

'They don't have to be! All they have to do is meet some of them bastards on the street of a night. It could be tonight, for all you know.'

I let it go. After the nine o'clock news, Alistair Cooke read his *Letter from America.* My husband loves that programme. And he said, as he always says: 'If I knew when

I was a young lad what I know now, I'd have taken passage to America. The land of opportunity, not like this godforsaken kip of a country.'

After that we listened to *We Beg to Differ* but he was annoyed that there were more women than men on the programme and he stamped off to bed when I refused to argue with him. I listened through to the end. Joyce Grenfell was one of the women. I saw her years ago in a film called *The Lamp Still Burns*. Then I left *The Friday Recital* playing low in the background and read Paul's letter.

Dear Julie.

I hope this letter finds you well and happy and that the possibility of a trip to London (and thence to Leamington) is still on the cards. What about a Christmas visit to your children? Indeed, they and you would be most welcome here for Christmas or Boxing Day or New Year's Eve?

You told me you grew up in the village of Moone. What a beautiful name for a birthplace. I've been thinking about that a lot and scribbling some lines which I attach. They were written and revised between serving customers in the shop. It's been a most busy time since Hallowe'en – for which I'm eternally grateful to the book buyers of Warwickshire.

You are on my mind. In my mind. I relive our few days together. I would love to spend more time with you. Easy, I know, for me to say, not being married and not being weighed down with Catholic guilt.

Write soon,
Paul

I smiled. Did he really believe Catholicism is keeping me here? I'll put him straight on that. I turned to the second page he'd sent a poem.

Moon Woman

The woman in the moon sets his heart on fire.
Her smile lifts the weight of the world from his shoulders.
Her breath kisses his neck while he is sleeping
and the beat of her distant heart
is perfectly in time with the beat of his own.
Someday, he knows, he'll live with her
on the shore of a tranquil sea.

Sunday, November 12

What do I say in replying to Paul? I tell him that it's not Catholic guilt that keeps me here; I tell him about the ragged band who attend the country Mass on Sundays; I tell him about the fear inside me, the fear my children have overcome in leaving; I tell him about the fact that I despise my husband and I'm not entirely sure why; I tell him I love getting his letters; I thank him for his poem; I say I wish I could write a poem for him; I tell him I'll borrow some poetry books from the library and familiarise myself with poems; I tell him my word of the day in my dictionary is *dragon*; I tell him I'm not breathing fire; I describe his shop as I imagine it; I ask if the canal in Leamington is anything like the canal here; I tell him the weather has been wet and wild; I tell him the wind has whipped the river and canal into waves and almost turned the tide of the river's flow; I tell him about a stick I threw in the water this morning which had hardly moved a foot in twenty minutes, such was the power of the wind; I tell him I'll write again soon.

I want to, but I don't, tell him I miss him.

Saturday, November 18

I woke this morning feeling really unwell. Creaking bones, headache, not able to raise my head from the pillow. After he'd had his breakfast, my husband came back up to the bedroom. 'You're not getting up?'

'I'm sick.'

'A cold?'

I nodded.

'Begob, I hope it's not the dose your mother had,' he said and then he was gone, out into the cold, wet morning, and I hated him even more.

Later, I woke to the sound of the radio downstairs and his shuffling feet on the stairs.

'I brung you up a cup of tea.' He left the mug on the bedside table. 'Would you like a cut of bread?'

'No, thanks.'

'Right. I'll leave you to rest.'

Sometimes I try to feel sorry for him, even as I hate him. He has his aspirations, I know, of getting away from the water, of buying that small farm. If I won the sweepstake, I'd buy him a farm and let him go. But we all have our disappointments and tragedies and losses and we don't drown them at the bottom of a pint glass. And we try to keep a kindness in our hearts and words.

Sunday, November 19

I felt this morning as though I would die.

My husband brought me tea and then disappeared to Mass. He got back here at five and stumbled up to bed at nine. The reek of stout filled the room. I went and lay in Margaret's bed and shivered for hours, feeling, again, that I might die.

Tuesday, November 21

I did not die.

I came downstairs and made some tea and toast and sat at the window, wrapped well against the cold. The rain has gone on falling for four days and the river has risen. Outside, the birds were huddled on the branches of the apple and the damson trees and in the little shelter offered by the ditches.

I thought about the birds who nest and sit in the trees around the cemetery at home. I used to imagine that birds were the souls of the dead returned, but now I think, perhaps, they're just attracted by the sadness and quietness of certain places. Is that why the trees and bushes around here are always filled with the still figures of crows, starlings and sparrows in winter?

Birds live on that note between ecstasy and oblivion. As do we.

Wednesday, November 22

Suddenly, this afternoon, there is sky where no sky was before. The branches form these peculiar, unexpected scratches on the heavens; their last few leaves have been gouged overnight by the wind from the east.

And the crows flitter down, like remnants of a dark cloud; their wings are blown shapeless as they fall, then rise, on sudden squalls that come hard on the gusty eastern wind.

And then they land and, heads low, graze the small, secluded River Field, below the winter ditch, their backs hunched taut against the raw and bleeding sleet. White stones, black forms pecking and hurrying from place to place.

Thursday, November 30

I long for the lost wildness in my world.

I walk to the Long Field and feed carrots and an apple to the workhorse. The sound of his chewing is a comfort to me, the natural world whispering to be of good heart.

Friday, December 1

I've always loved Christmas and the Christmas season. December and May are my favourite months. May because the summer begins to appear from behind the hedges and beneath the ground. December because the Christmas season is at the heart of it.

When I was a child, though the country was at war, my parents and then my father alone made a festival of the month. It was all building up to a visit to Castledermot on the eighth of December. Once Mass was over, we'd head for the town, me on the carrier behind my father, his heavy coat keeping the wind off my face. The place was always full of people: corner boys on the square; shopkeepers in their doorways; head-scarved women hurrying homeward; children waiting for whatever excitement the day might throw their way; farmers looking uneasy in their Sunday suits.

And we'd stand outside the windows of Cope's shop and examine every toy on display. And then we'd have our dinner in McEvoy's eating house. Afterwards, it was back to the windows for a second look and an enquiry about what Santa might be asked to bring. And then the slow cycle home as dusk began to fall.

When Margaret and Robert were small, their excitement was contagious. Even during the Emergency, the thought of Christmas, the toys in shop windows, the visits to the crib, my father always finding something special for them, made every day an adventure once we reached the eighth of the month.

Strange that my childhood and theirs were lived at times of war and yet it's the Christmases and the excitement and the holly above the door and the paper streamers in the kitchen and the carols in the church and the smell of dry straw in the crib that are so strong, even still. Nothing can spoil that sense. Nothing and nobody.

I wonder what Christmas will be like in London. I wonder what Christmas would be like in Leamington.

When I went to work in Waterford as a girl, Christmas was all about the bustle in the shop, the warm eyes in cold faces, the excitement of buying presents, the sense that the world was filled with expectation, wonder and joy and opportunity. A shop was the best place to be then. Everyone who came and went brought that feeling of celebration with them. And after work the streets were filled with voices and music and light and ... Christmas. It was as if the season could be touched and felt and tasted and heard whether you were in a city or in the country.

And then the Christmas Eve train back to Maganey or Athy and my father waiting, his bike and mine propped against the station wall. The foostering and fumbling to get my case secured onto the carrier and then full pelt home. And the dressing up for midnight Mass and the callers, afterwards, to the house, and falling into bed exhausted but full with the knowledge that this had only been Christmas Eve and tomorrow would be another day of ease and joy. And last thing, before I slept, I'd whisper: 'Good night, my lovely mother, wherever you are.'

Tuesday, December 5

I watched and listened as a mistle thrush sat in a red-berried holly bush along the edge of the Low Field. Around the song there was an absolute silence in the afternoon, nothing stirring, not a ripple on the shiny leaves of the holly. It was an afternoon that whispered *winter*.

Once or twice I looked up into the falling twilight, imagining and willing snow to tumble amidst the hush of wintertime.

The mistle thrush sang his song. It rang out clear and warm across the field and then it seemed to echo in the Rush Field, as though it had bounced against the stone walls and back again. And its tune was beautiful and brave. It didn't seem to care who heard and the music in its singing was sweet and lifted my heart.

Come February, if the weather is right, the mistle thrushes will breed and there will be a dozen singers in the ditch between the fields.

Friday, December 8

Carlow was teeming with people today. And so the season begins. No war. No bombing of Britain. No soldiers on the streets. A time of peace. But each of us carries with us our own war and uncertainty and regret.

I did my shopping and, when I got home, I wrapped Margaret and Robert's presents. Tomorrow I'll post them. I wonder whether they'll miss home this Christmas. I think not. How could they? The arguments, the sniping remarks, the drunken nights that move from Sunday to Thursday, Friday, Saturday and Sunday.

No doubt they'll miss the chatting after midnight Mass. They may even think about how they'd have met their school friends in the churchyard, told them about life in London, heard stories of how those friends' lives were going, arranged to meet on Stephen's Day before they'd catch the train and boat back to England. But missing that will be a small price to pay for missing all the rest.

Will I miss them? Of course I will. This will be my first Christmas in twenty years with just my husband for company, if company is the word. With just the pair of us in the house. Let the weather be dry!

Monday, December 11

A letter came from Paul. A letter and a Christmas card. The picture on the card is of a cottage in the country. The ground is deep in snow but there's a horse and wagon passing and a boy and girl standing at the cottage door, waving to the wagoner. And the wagoner is waving back. Above them a big full moon is sitting in a starry sky. Inside, Paul wrote: *Not Ireland and not Leamington but, perhaps, a dream come true. Wishing you a happy and peaceful Christmas wherever you are. Paul.*

The full moon here will come on Christmas Eve.

Paul's letter suggests, again, that I should think of visiting the children. He offers to pay my fare. He says he can telegraph the money to me. He says that if I take this step, it will make it easier to take the next step and the next. He says the steps don't need to lead to him but, only, away from unhappiness. He says he misses me and that our two days together were the happiest and most fulfilling days of his life.

It's raining here. I hope the rain will clear for Christmas and that the frost arrives with a cleansing vengeance.

Wednesday, December 13

The rain has gone on falling for the fourth consecutive day. At breakfast I said this and my husband looked at me and snarled: 'Would you not, for fuck's sake, say "the fourth day in a row"? Where the hell did you get this consecutive stuff? In that book your father gave you? You were a shop girl, not a bloody teacher. Just because your father thought you were a princess doesn't mean you'll ever be queen, you know that?'

With those words he was gone, out into the pelting rain. I laughed. I have never imagined he could string sentences like that together and finish with such a well-turned image.

And still the rain goes on and on. For the fourth consecutive day!

In the afternoon I walked to the Long Field. The lower part is flooded and the workhorse has moved to the higher land above the chestnut tree. I called and he came splashing through the flood water. His reward was three apples. He nodded, chewed the apples and then trotted back to the shelter of the high ditch.

Friday, December 15

A glorious evening of heavy frost and, even in the dim light of the first quarter of the moon, the countryside is lit up with jewels. So I have come into my Christmas kingdom, despite what my husband thinks.

I wrote to Margaret and Robert and reminded them that Christmas Eve and Christmas night will bring a full moon and I told them I'd stand outside at midnight, in the hope of clear skies, and look at the moon and know they were looking at it, too. And, in that way, we'd be together.

But tonight is everything I hope for from the season. The sky is clear and filled with stars. The leafless trees along the opposite bank are sketched against the canvas of the night. There's a stillness like death. I think of my mother laid out on her bed thirty-one years ago. The wracking, drowning cough is stopped. The silence is like a thanksgiving for the end of pain. Before she died, her face turned blue. The nurse told us afterwards that she'd seen that happen to so many people, drowning in the fluid that flooded their lungs. I say a prayer for her, an unbeliever's prayer: 'Mother, if you have a memory, remember me as I remember you.'

And then I walk on. The river runs quietly beside me. An owl calls out like a train in the night and then another answers from across the river and I stand and listen to the call and reply and I imagine small animals trembling in the ditches and dykes at that sound, knowing the danger it brings. And I think of the night trains rumbling through the stations at Maganey and Athy. And I think of my father, his body stretched cold for this first Christmas in death, and I miss him and miss the comfort of his being there should I need him.

Saturday, December 16

Long letters come from Margaret and Robert. Long letters meant to be read by my husband and me. I read him their news at the supper table. They tell us they can't get time off at Christmas, or not enough to travel home and get back for work. They say they'll miss us and to tell everyone they said hello and happy Christmas.

'Did they send any money?' my husband asks.

I hand him two English five-pound notes.

'They broke themselves,' he says. 'And who the hell is goin' to take them? They're not real Irish money at all.'

'I'll change them in the bank on Monday.'

'Did they send you anything?'

'The same,' I lie.

'Well that in itself.'

He slides the two five-pound notes back to me. I put them in the envelope.

'They seem to be doing all right,' he says.

'They do.'

And then we go on eating our meal.

I don't tell him about the single sheet of paper that came with the letters, words written in Margaret's neat hand: *I don't think we'll ever come home again. We hope you understand.*

I understand.

Monday, December 18

I woke this morning to a sky so low it seemed to be hardly higher than the rooftop. And then it came in the afternoon. Snow, snow, snow. My husband cursed the falling whiteness but I could hardly wait to get out into the blinding light of the afternoon, a light that danced and dodged between the trees in the Little Wood.

The evergreen oaks were overlaid with a heavy coat of paleness, their leaves and branches sagging under the weight of the falling flakes. The other trees, bare for winter, were suddenly radiant as their branches stretched like decorated arms in every direction. I stood in a small clearing between the sycamores and turned my face to the falling sky.

Down it came, growing heavier as the darkness fell with it.

Was it falling, I wondered, in Leamington? Was it falling on the Cotswold Hills? Was it falling between the tall buildings onto London's streets? And then I returned to the here and now, to the soft rise and fall of the land as I traipsed back home, not wanting to be indoors, not wanting to miss the cold dryness of the flecks and patches that were tumbling through the fall of night.

In the Low Field, I found fox tracks in the snow, light as the flurries through which the animal had passed. A vixen. I've seen her skirt our garden and, sometimes, venture in between the apple and the damson trees in search of food. I followed her tracks, down the fall of the little hill, along the shelter of the hedge and there they disappeared into the thickness of the brambles.

I am sitting now at the kitchen window. The house is in darkness. The curtains are open and I am waiting for the vixen to pass again, on her way back home. And still the snow is falling.

I have just written to Paul, describing as best I can the beauty here on this night in Christmas week. And I finished the letter by telling him I missed him and wishing we could be together, walking side by side through deep, white fields. And then I sealed the envelope, for fear I'd change my mind and dilute what I had written.

Tuesday, December 19

The minute breakfast was over, I pulled on my coat and boots and set off for the wood again. The snow had stopped falling but the sky promised more. I crossed the little patch where the babies are buried; the white stones are nowhere to be seen. I thought of what Paul said about taking their memory with me but I know that when the snow clears their graves will still be there.

As I climbed to the Little Wood, the clouds fractured for a moment and a shaft of sunlight hit one of the evergreens and it became a Christmas tree, fitting for the season. All its summer brightness was gone but it seemed to sing out in jubilation, saluting winter and the winter sun.

Thursday, December 21

Midwinter's Day and slowly the year will turn its back on the waning of the light, its face to all that lies ahead. And I stand here, my shoulders against the wind and rain that has begun to wash away the snow, my face towards the lifting sun.

Everything begins again: this joy; this life; these days; this love I feel for someone far away.

Saturday, December 23

The stones around the children's graves are dull and grubby after the whiteness of the snowfall. I place two wreaths of holly on the graves and stand to think about my lost children, dead and living.

A robin in the leafless hedge sings out her song. No bird should have the energy to sing on this damp, bleak day but sing she does. In wind, in snow, in rain, in hope against the bitter wind. In celebration of her life, her courage, her unborn children. And mine, I like to think.

Sunday, December 24

This Christmas Eve I saw three things.

I saw a dead fox on the road outside the town.

I saw a gravedigger climbing over the cemetery wall with his spade, shovel and pickaxe wrapped in sacks.

I saw a robin sitting on one of the white stones my husband placed above the babies' graves and I wanted to tell him, but he was nowhere to be found.

Monday, December 25

Christmas dawned behind the hill, its fire rising in the sky, and day was opened like a gift laid before the sleeping infant Jesus.

I cycled to early Mass. The day was grey but the rain had stopped. As I leaned my bicycle against the side wall of the chapel, The Man in the Cap appeared as though from thin air.

'Good morning, ma'am,' he said. 'May I wish you the blessings of the season.'

I had never heard him speak and never seen him materialise before the start of Mass but there he was. I was so surprised, I hesitated before answering.

'What I mean is to wish you a happy Christmas, ma'am, and a time of good peace in your heart.'

'Thank you,' I said. 'And a very happy and peaceful Christmas to you.'

'Now, I'll make myself scarce till the priest has proceedings underway,' The Man in the Cap said, smiling. 'I wouldn't want himself getting the idea that I'd break the habit of a lifetime.' With that, he was gone but, sure enough, he appeared in the church just as the opening prayers were done.

The day passed. My husband and I raised a glass to our absent children and, in the afternoon, we listened to the radio. First to Ted Ray and, later, to *The Great Gilhooly* and Christmas songs and *The Linden Tree*. And, God forgive me, I resented the fact that my husband sat in silence and laughed occasionally or hummed along with a Christmas song.

When *The Linden Tree* ended, he yawned and stretched and said: 'Well, that's another Christmas over and done. It wasn't a bad day, was it?'

'No,' I said.

'Sure we rub along all right even without the children.'

'We do,' I lied.

'I'll head on up to bed. Tomorrow is another day.'

'I'll be up in a while.'

'I might go into town and have a couple of pints with the boys after the dinner tomorrow.'

I nodded.

'Goodnight, so,' he said.

'Goodnight,' I said.

He stopped in the doorway. 'I'll paint the little stones around the graves in the morning. They look a bit lost after the snow and the rain.'

'Thank you.'

And then he was gone up the creaking stairs and I hated him even more for this small act of kindness.

Is that another mark of insanity? My inability to take even a tiny kindness and be grateful for it? Or am I just immune to anything positive at this stage in our lives?

I smile. The doctor who put me away used a similar phrase. 'It's something that happens to a lot of women at this time in their life,' he said. And then I think about the women I shared the ward with in The Mental. And I think about the book-keeper and his hands. And I wish them all what The Man in the Cap wished me, a time of good peace in their hearts.

Sunday, December 31

There's an inevitable disappointment to this season but there's a bitterness, too, in my heart at the year gone by and at my own state. Like the fields and water puddles outside, I'm frozen.

I look back on the year and I see my two living children fled to London. I'm glad for them and envy them their youth and the possibilities they have. I can only hope they don't make the same mistakes I did, confusing a glittery waistcoat for happiness. I have no one to blame but myself. I wasn't raised to be a magpie, to fall for the first shiny thing that caught my eye. The night before my wedding, my father asked me if I was sure I was doing the right thing. I said I was. But he didn't let it go. We were sitting at the kitchen table in our house.

He looked me straight in the eye and said: 'It wouldn't be the end of anyone's world if you wanted to think some more about this. No one who really matters would be put out by that.'

'It's the right thing,' I said.

Now I wonder what I meant by right – right for me or right in the eyes of the world or right for my husband? It wasn't right for me, but I didn't know that back then. I suspect my father did but he was too gentle a man to say it, for fear of upsetting me. All he could do was plant the question in my head. But I was a young woman of twenty-two; the thought of a house and a husband and children and the freedom to do as we pleased was all that filled my mind. I was, to be truthful, as empty-headed as my husband, so I can't blame him entirely. We both said *I do*. He for his reasons and I for mine.

How would it be to sit some evening across our table and ask him what his reasons were and when it was they faded and what he thinks of our life now? But that will never happen. Either he'd walk away or, more than likely, he'd shout and rant about how I'm never happy and have ideas above my station and can I not be content with who I am and what makes a shop girl think she should ever be anything better?

I hope my children have more sense than I did. I hope the wreck that is my marriage, a ruin they've seen at close quarters, is warning enough to them to take their time in finding a road towards whatever happiness the world might have to offer.

And I look back at my time in The Mental. Those few months in the spring of this year. How easy it was to have me wiped off the face of the earth. How willing the doctor, the guard and the priest were to help my husband make nothing of my life.

The only kindness I found at that time was among the doctors and the nurses and the patients in that other world behind the thirty-foot walls. Nothing that was said or done in there could ever come close to the cruelty of the one who put me away. And for what? For wandering in the night. For stepping onto a train. For not being sure of who I was or what or where I wanted to be. That was my crime. That and causing my husband embarrassment.

Nothing that was said or done inside the walls of The Mental was as cruel as the things that were said and done within the walls of this house, but they count for nothing. They're part and parcel of the life in which I am expected to live.

But the year gone by has had its brightness, too. My children flying the limits of this harsh and punishing nest was a good thing. Paul's barge easing through the lock and mooring for the night and all that followed were good things. The fact that I felt and feel no guilt about those days is a good thing. So many things for which to be grateful. And I thank myself for having the courage to let my two children go, for the courage to go in search of myself again.

In the autumn and winter of last year, I resisted the temptation to step into the river and let it carry me away. I felt I couldn't face the Christmas lights but, because the children were still here at the time, I avoided the riverbank.

How different that was from the first year I spent here, the first spring after we were married. Everything about the house was new to me and I wanted so much to make it my own. My husband came in from work one evening laughing.

'I didn't know I married a painter,' he said.

And then, the first weeks of that spring brought the daffodils flooding the bank – remnants of other lives, of the men and women who had lived in this house in the past, images from history spearing the spring mornings, and I realised that this house would never be fully ours. It would always partly belong to the ghosts of the women and men who had lived here in the past, and that thought brought me a strange satisfaction.

1951

Monday, January 1

A cold, pure day with a blue sky above and frosted earth below. A day to clear the mind and to imagine that the future can be seen. Imagine or pretend. For today, I settled on imagine. I was walking to the Little Wood and, as I followed the paths and openings through the ditches, I got to thinking of maps. I made a map in my head of the places I have been. The map begins at Moone, where I was born and grew up. It follows roads to Castledermot and Athy and once or twice to Dublin. It leads me to Waterford for work and Maganey railway station where I met my husband. It brings me here to this house on the bank of the Barrow river and the canal. And that is the extent of my travels. I have been to seven counties in my life: Kildare, Dublin, Carlow, Wicklow, Laois, Kilkenny and Waterford. That is the extent of my tiny life. I am more than forty years old and, but for work, I would never have stepped outside the province of Leinster. I read books, I travel in my mind, but I am not a traveller.

As always, the arrival of a new year set my mind wondering about the future, and today, sitting in the cold wood above the river and the house, staring into the blue sky and watching as the marks of my footsteps began to freeze into the falling light of afternoon, I wondered where the map might take me in the coming year.

On this day last year, I never dreamed I'd be in The Mental in a matter of weeks but I was. So if I don't dream of London or Leamington, if I don't dream of opening the door some summer afternoon and finding Paul standing outside, might I go to those places, might I see his face again and touch the grey curls on his head?

The new year brings new hopes.

Wednesday, January 3

Last night I had a strange dream. Strange because there was no hint of imagination in it. The dream was exactly as the event happened. It was the year after we married and my husband had brought home the local paper as a treat for me. Those were the days when he didn't sneer at my love of words. I remember him telling a cousin of his, with pride in his voice, that 'Julie is the greatest reader you could meet. The sure sign of a bright woman.' Does he regret that now, I wonder?

In the dream, I was sitting at the kitchen table leafing through the news when my eyes fell on a report of a court case in which a woman, in a town in the county of my birth, was charged with attempted suicide. The details of the case outlined that because she had young children and had *wilfully put them in danger of becoming motherless*, she should be sentenced to three months' imprisonment. I reread the report, thinking there must be some mistake, but the story was as I'd read it.

I woke at four o'clock. The room was pitch dark, my husband sleeping the sleep of the unjust beside me. I went downstairs and made some tea and thought about the woman in the dream, the woman in the court report. She was forty-four years old. Was that why I dreamt of her, because I am now, more or less, of an age with her?

The dream upset me greatly. I couldn't go back to sleep or to bed. Is she still alive? She could well be; she'd be sixty-five now. Is she still living in the shadow of that jail sentence, of that newspaper report, of the shame and humiliation of being locked up in prison for attempting to take her own life?

The lesson is: if you wish to do such a thing, do it well. And my own lesson is: if you wish to step out of line, do it well, too. Step so far out of line that you won't be seen.

Friday, January 12

I spent the late afternoon pruning trees. It was a typical January afternoon with the wind coming in from the Ridge and my hands freezing in the chilly air. By the time I'd finished, the orchard shadows were stretching towards the creeping in of night. I found the final fruit of last year's crop, high in a corner tree, its bee-sucked skin a parchment around memory. That apple, filled with the possibilities of every summer yet to come, seemed to have ripened again in the rays of the waning sun.

In my stupidity, I told my husband what I'd thought. He said: 'You're startin' to sound like an Englishwoman out of one of them books you do be readin'.'

For a second, I thought he might have found one of Paul's letters but, when I checked, nothing had been touched.

Sunday, January 14

Passing the Long Field, I met the farmer who owns it. He had been up to check on the workhorse.

'Not looking good,' he told me when I asked how the animal was faring. 'His time is near or near enough.'

'I'm sorry to hear that.'

'He was a good beast. Never let me down. He's twenty-nine. A good age.'

'Let's hope he'll see another summer.'

'We'll see. I wouldn't put him through anything more than he can bear.'

Thursday, January 18

I woke to the dark whiteness of a window pasted with snow. The new year blows in where the old crept out with ice, the waxing moon laid low upon its back.

I had the stolen pleasure of Christmas cake at dinner time, a misdemeanour against my best new year resolution.

It's nine o'clock in the evening and, outside, snow pricks the pewter sky and the old heavens hold their breath. In a day or two, the rain will fly in and wash all this away. But, for this moment, seated here, soft flakes upon the window pane, all might be well and a childhood Christmas might have come again. Come to wrap me up in kindness against the grey that will fetch in another day of brutal hail, another morning humped against the fading light of early afternoon.

Why can't I live in the day of snow light, instead of running always to the darker places and times I imagine to be around the corner? If I could answer that question, would I be a different woman? Would I live another life?

Monday, January 22

A letter comes from Leamington.

Dear Julie,

My profound apologies for the long delay in writing. I hope your Christmas and New Year were times of celebration and rest. I spent Christmas Day with my sister and her family in the Cotswolds, in a village called Moreton-in-Marsh. It was a quiet time and enjoyable but I was glad to get back to my own rambling rooms on Boxing Day.

I would have written then but, on December 28, the young man who worked with me in the bookshop was found dead. He had taken his own life. His name was Brian. He was twenty-three years old, a quiet, beautiful young man. He had faced his demons – many of them created by other people. When we last spoke, on Christmas Eve, he told me a number of his former school friends had taken to making fun of him because of his homosexuality. He laughed about it but I knew there was an aching that he couldn't seem to express and a pain he was trying valiantly to hide.

We agreed to talk again after the Christmas holiday and I told him he could telephone me at any time, at my sister's house or my own. No call came. And then, on the Thursday afternoon, he was found dead in a reservoir near here. He had left a note for his family and one for me. He thanked me for my friendship.

All I could think was that, had I been as good a friend as he needed, he would have telephoned or come and seen me.

I don't believe I have ever been so affected by a death. I've lost my own parents and a number of friends over the years but there was something about this which was wanton, cruel and needless. I was angry with the young men who had driven him to that end but, mostly, I was angry with death. Death which is blind and deaf, whose wordless word is always final. Death is a scavenger rustling near a flooded dyke, stalking the winter headlands dressed in snow; a muscular stranger on a summer beach, eyeing the bodies of sun-drenched girls, a swimmer just a stroke too far from shore. It carries a snigger camouflaged as a smile and has a mouth of lipstick sweetness. Its bite is far more vicious than its bark. It's devoid of imagination and has but one idea, stolen from a falling angel.

I have grown to personalise and hate it in these past few weeks.

I'm sorry to burden you with such dark lines but I needed to write them down, to try to expel the blackness from my mind. Not to pass it on to you but to share these thoughts which have been my sleeping and waking companions.

I have some small sense now of what you meant when you spoke about your children and how much a part of you they are and how much you feel the need to be with them. This young man came into my life as an employee three years ago and I like to think he became a friend too. His presence, even in his absence, is so much a part of this shop. It's there between the bookshelves, on every aisle and on the turn of the stair and will be for as long as I can imagine.

On a brighter note, and heaven knows we need a brighter note, we are just over a week from the first day of spring. Better days lie ahead and after spring comes summer with all its promise and possibility.

I hope you are well. I hope the sunnier days are just around the corner for you – for all of us. And I hope to see you in the months ahead.

I wrote back to Paul, saying whatever I could. I'm not sure my words are enough – I never am – but they're the best I have to offer.

Tuesday, January 23

After dinner, I cycled to town to post my letter to Paul. I called in to the bookshop and bought *A Town Like Alice* by Neville Shute, one of the little luxuries accruing from my selling bread to the bargemen. By the time I was ready to leave, darkness had fallen. On my way home, I saw an extraordinary thing. Passing a small house on the edge of the town, the wintry evening beginning to settle about me, I noticed a window quick with light. The curtains hadn't been drawn and I could see a woman, a cello in her grasp in the small cottage room. I was mystified and delighted by the sight.

I got down from my bike and stood on the road outside, beyond the light from the window. And then the woman sat and began to play but the music went unheard for me. I imagined all the notes entangled in that crowded space, like dandelion clocks rising in the evening air, the cellist stock still, only her fingers stirring.

Cycling away, I dreamt an octave higher: the year spread out with summer light, unhurried music drifting from the opened window across a sun-drenched afternoon and, all the way home, I had the joy of the remembered sight and the rich, imagined sound.

Wednesday, January 31

The last day of winter.

A storm is coming down the river, crowding through the arches of the bridge.

The swans have taken to the rushes, their necks and heads a glimpse of snow between the battered greenery. And, farther up, the sheep have folded into the shelter of the hill, heads low, rumps against the wind.

For now, the Barrow waters are backed up, dark waves bucking against the wintry light, warnings of the sea and what the river will become when it has run its deep, unsettled course.

On days like this, I feel I am teetering on the edge of the world and the edge of life, looking in, looking on.

Friday, February 2

As I was standing at the kitchen table this morning, making bread, I thought of Paul's young friend, Brian, and then I thought of what he had written about sensing his absence as a presence in the bookshop. And I stood very still and listened for some sense of those who lived here and have left us. But there was nothing. No creak on the floor above, no scent of perfume, no sound that might have been a barely perceptible laugh.

And then I thought of the swallows, perhaps because today is the second day of spring. I wondered whether swallows ever dream of summers here. Are those dreams a map that is a part of how they find their way back to us year after year?

Wednesday, February 14

The third day of rain. The river is rising.

There are floods in the meadows all about us, one field leaking into another.

I hate the rain. I hate the way the black skies come down to smother the trees and ditches and gateposts and even the path between the apple trees. I heard Paul Robeson on the radio singing 'All the world am sad and dreary, everywhere I roam'. Today the world is a dark place.

I write a long letter to Margaret and Robert. I write to Paul and wish him better thoughts and brighter days ahead. I don't mention the floods, the rain, the darkness, the feeling of despair that lies inside and out.

Today is the anniversary of the death of one of my little babies. I wrap up against the wind and rain and climb through the gap in the hedge and stand beside the graves and cry.

Thursday, February 15

After all this rain, the Little River has appeared again. This is only the third time I've seen it above ground in all my years of living here. Its singing voice is like a bass note between the granite rocks that mark its invisible course from year to year. And then there's a lighter music over stones, and all this beneath the brambles in their winter green.

Monday, February 19

It snowed all last night. So much for spring. But I was glad to see it come. A brightness after weeks of rain and cloud and mist and greyness.

The snow is stuffed in gaps and gateways, like old rags.

We are guests on earth. We have no say beyond the little things.

On the hill below the wood, the fog is moving like ghosts.

Wednesday, February 21

Today is my birthday. I am forty-five years old. I am a woman looking out over the garden from the window of a bedroom. Downstairs there are two cards on the mantelpiece. One from my daughter and one from my son. At dinner time my husband said, 'Happy birthday, Julie. The pair of us is gettin' on but, sure, we still kick up a bit of dust.' It was the first time he had used my name since Christmas.

Years ago, when he first asked my name, I said, 'Julie McDermot – with one t.'

It became his standing joke when he introduced me to his friends.

'Her family ran out of tea,' he'd say and his friends would laugh. Not all of them but some.

Sunday, February 25

While my husband sleeps upstairs, I write to Paul:

This week the fields have changed their clothes and the shadows lengthen in our lives and then our lives are gone. But you are the break of day.

There's nothing else I want or need to say and so I leave it at that. I know he'll understand.

Thursday, March 1

My second reappearing cottage. My spring cottage. This one is on the Mill Lane and it reappears in bitter March, emerging from the overgrowth of briars and branches before disappearing again into the growth of spring. Its doorway is a gaping hole into a sepulchre. The scent of pipe smoke hangs like the scent of herbs in the brittle air and I imagine the ghost of the long-dead smoker at my shoulder.

I think of him, not Lazarus-like but like the resurrected Jesus, come to lean against the sloping wall; his shoulder holds the house in place, his hand blue-washing the brittle stone. I visualise his ghost eyes taking in the garden long gone to seed, to weed, to wilderness.

In the mesh and muddle of branches behind the cottage is the remnant of a bower where there must have been a seat and roses that blushed beside the gate. I imagine the pipe-smoker smile his phantom smile and I know spring is truly about to leap.

On my way home, I cycle to the sand pit, leave my bicycle inside the gate and cross to the Long Field. The workhorse stands beside the chestnut tree, almost leaning against it for support. I climb the gate, cross the damp grass and rub his face and mane. His eyes are closed and they stay closed. I talk to him. I tell him I'll be thinking of him.

Monday, March 12

The workhorse died this morning. I met his owner on the road and he stopped to tell me,

'Drifted off. A good way to go. I was up to him twice a day. Found him dead this morning, under the chestnut. We'll bury him in the field after the dinner hour. Lived there, died there. It's only right that he'll be buried there.'

In the afternoon, I went and stood at the gate of the Long Field, watching as three men and the farmer dug the horse's grave and then they tied chains around his huge frame and pulled it gently behind a tractor, rolling it slowly into the hole.

While the men closed the grave, the farmer came and stood with me.

'You were fond of him,' he said. 'I often seen you feeding him apples and I passing.'

He foostered in the pocket of his coat and produced the horse's ring bit. 'Would you like this? As a memory, sort of?'

I could see he was embarrassed by what others might perceive as a softness.

I took the jointed metal from him. 'I'd love it. And I thank you.'

'I better get back and see that these fellows are doing it proper.' He turned to go.

'Did the horse have a name?' I asked.

'Billy,' he said. 'And then Old Billy.'

'What the fuck do you want with that dirty thing in the house?' my husband asks when he sees the ring bit on the kitchen table.

Tuesday, March 13

The potatoes are in the ground. My husband stands at the head of the last drill and surveys his day's work.

A week ago, when he began the turning of the soil, I brought him tea and he stopped his work and said: 'I'm peelin' back the sod to find the clay again and all that means.'

My heart sank for the lost farmer in him.

Sunday, March 25

Easter Sunday. Fifteen years ago I'd have spent hours painting eggs for the children and hiding them in the garden.

Today is a true March day – wind, rain, cold, the sky sitting no more than fifty feet above the river. The bottom end of the Low Field has been lying in a misty fog all day.

I put on my coat and walked in search of some sign of resurrection in the land, but today there was none. Winter has returned, as it so often does in March, sneaking in under cover of darkness and waiting for the world's people to pull back their curtains and sigh.

My husband was very late back from town and rambling drunk. I had to help him up the stairs. At the top step I wondered whether I shouldn't leave him in a heap on the landing, pack a case and cycle back to Moone and stay there. But I didn't. Julie McDermot did the right thing. Again. Julie McDermot did the wrong thing. Again. Julie McDermot has no idea what she's doing.

Tuesday, March 27

Last week I wrote to Paul, hoping he was well and that Brian's ghost was sleeping more easily. Today his letter came.

Dear Julie,

You ask about Brian's ghost. You know, I cannot shake his memory from me at all. I carry a feeling of guilt with me through most days.

His parents called to the shop just last week and we sat and chatted about him. They tried to reassure me that there was nothing more I could have done, that he had set his own course and was, in the end, not for turning. We even laughed a little about him and his foibles. They didn't mention his homosexuality and nor did I – it was as if the truth were there, like him, just beyond the circle of our conversation.

I thought of the vicar who conducted Brian's funeral service and how the picture he painted was not of the young man I knew; the picture was even more of an illusion than his ghost.

Often, it seems, the truth earns punishments more painful than a lie and all the side-of-the-mouth talk of honesty and openness is just a song for singing at the grave. Enter the druids and the mystics in their fluid gowns of gold, the witches and the warlocks who go back to childhood rites. They all appear out of the ether with their prattling tongues and bogus voices – the messengers of certainty. I have no fear of these self-righteous holy men because I have no time for them.

Where once I thought myself a heretic, I know now there was nothing to believe. It's all about accoutrements: the costume cut for performance; fear of the unknown as a kind of crucifix. Let these holy men, of all persuasions, display these trinkets if they wish. I have no use for them. No use, no time, no need – I am, again, a fully convinced unbeliever.

Do I sound as though I've gone off the deep end? I ask only because you would tell me; you're the expert in that field. That is my little joke!

I miss your common sense, Julie. I miss your grounded earthiness. I miss your Irishness, your openness, your courage to be true. How well you were named. Beautiful, soft-haired, youthful, isn't that what the name means? Your letter came like a balm to me. You are the sun and I am the moon. I think back to last summer and it seems as though we spent so long together. What was it? Two days. Does it seem that way to you, so little yet so wonderful a time?

The courage to be true! Do I have the courage to be true? Is staying here a truth to my lost children or a fear of the world and a fear of myself?

And I think of the men – and maybe the women, too – who are behind the walls of The Mental for being like Paul's young friend. The people we do not understand and see as a threat to *normal life* are the ones we lock away. God – normal society's God – forbid that people might be infected by any kind of difference.

Monday, April 2

A glorious day of sunshine and heat. This morning, I walked to the wood and picked some early forget-me-nots and made three small bunches. The first I laid on Old Billy's grave. The mound is settling and sinking, as is he, back into the heart of the land. The other bunches I placed on the babies' graves. Some people would think it an obscenity, no doubt, to place a posy on a horse's grave and then place posies on the graves of children. We are all living things. They were all living things.

In the evening, I walked the bank and revisited the spot where Paul tied up the barge, the spot where we sat and ate and talked. And when I got back, I sat on the wall of the lock, my feet dangling above the water, where we lay together on the barge that night.

Darkness fell but the night continued warm. In the end, my husband came to the garden gate and called me.

'What the hell would you want sittin' out of a night like this?' he asked. 'You'll get your death of cold.'

Are his words a consideration or just a habit?

Wednesday, April 18

Almost two weeks without rain and two weeks of summer weather.

Soon, the sandpit will be a madness of swallows. April is posing as July. Time enough to judge the summer come September, when the swallows fly away again.

On my way back home, a breeze catches the early cherry blossoms. Cerise and white, they rise above the tree, then fall. Roadway and path are littered now with petals, flowers folded below the garden wall like forgotten confetti.

Sunday, April 22

I found a starling dead on the road near the church. Sometimes the world wobbles on its axis and this is the way things work. One minute the starling is in carefree flight, her wings in love with the warm wind, her hymn a song of joy, eyes fixed on the flowering haw. And then a flounce of falling feathers, an unfinished song. Her small, precious heart less than the weight of empty skin and splintered bone. The world wobbling on its beautiful, awful axis.

Late in the evening the little birds come to the orchard to feed in the summery air.

The smallest bodies on the frailest wings. Sometimes they mutter in the damson tree, sometimes they sing, and often they are as silent as the sky about them. But once in a while, they speak to me, not in some wild, imagined tongue, not as the confraternity of St Francis, but in single words, short phrases, syllables even. I suppose I'd call their murmurings a kind of information, an odds-and-ends view of the world.

Tonight they said: *The truth will set you free and, if it doesn't, the truth will drive you mad.*

Sometimes the smallest voices speak the clearest truths.

Monday, April 30

There's something about the turning of the month, the turning of the season and the turning of the year that has always caught my fancy. This is the end of the last hour of April, and the first hour of May – the first hour of summer – is about to begin. And I have completed a year of freedom from my supposed madness.

Spring weds her summer under the cherries that are all astray in the midnight wind, their wild confetti in her hair. The breeze blows slow and warm. Which is the truer, heat or storm, the stiffness of the wind or the warmness of the air?

Which is the truer – staying or going, being or vanishing?

Tuesday, May 1

Dear Paul,

This is the first day of the first month of summer. Cherry blossom, lilac and the snowy whitethorn escort the season to my door. I feel like celebrating. We are almost back where we began, a year older and little the wiser, but eager to know what the future might bring.

I don't know what I can promise. I don't even think ahead to your possible visit because I know my husband will almost certainly be here when you come but I'll find a way around that. All I know is what I feel and today I feel like nothing else matters on earth.

I'm sitting in the garden. The sun is warm, the birds are singing, the trees are in flower, the world is right. I've been trying to imagine the streets of your town, the details of the quiet corners of your shop, the colour of the shop door, the trees and flowers in your garden, the places you walk.

My wishes for you are that you may walk in warm sunlight; that when you stop to speak, it is to friends; that when you rest, it is in the place you call home.

The bluebells are waving in the Little Wood, a single late daffodil is still blowing its trumpet in the corner of my garden, red poppies will shepherd in the bright days of July.

All these flowers, all these days and weeks stretch before us like the familiar streets of the town you love, filled with the smiling faces of those you know. And your visit lies ahead of us with whatever time we can snatch to be together.

The river is charged with life; the wild birds are singing in every tree.

Have I said enough? Do you understand?

The moment I had finished the letter, I sealed it in an envelope, addressed and stamped it and cycled to the postbox. I felt elated and uncertain. Had I said enough? Had I said too much?

Wednesday, May 2

All day I've had a sense of dread in my stomach, knowing my letter – my mad sunlit letter – is winging its way across the Irish Sea. The day is grey with spits and slops of rain – so unlike yesterday. Is the weather a reflection of my mood or is my mood a reflection of the weather?

Did I believe, as I sat and wrote, that anything will really change? Do I suppose, if Paul comes sailing down the river in August or September, that we'll find a time and place to be together, to touch, to kiss, to make love, while my husband sighs and grumbles about *these bloody English bargemen who don't know when summer ends*?

Madnesses and sadnesses chase me through my life.

In the afternoon I go up to the graves and place a branch of cherry blossom on each one and talk to the babies, asking their advice, begging their understanding for this urge to be away from here.

On my way back from the Little Wood, I notice that the cherry flowers are already flat and sad upon the graves.

Saturday, May 5

On a whim, I cycled back to Moone, returned to my home.

I took a route I haven't taken in years, out of Carlow, through Palatine, along the small roads that have lost their way, like my father's redundant medical prescription that still sits on the dresser, waiting to be filled.

I opened the house to the day, let the sunlight in and the winter air out. Two passing neighbours called. One asked: 'Would you consider moving back here, Julie?' I wasn't sure whether it was a genuine question or a roundabout way of enquiring whether I'd sell the house.

I made tea and sat in the yard and then I began the job of scuffling the weeds that have grown through the spring, making small mounds as I went. Later, I raked the weeds together into one big pile and barrowed them to the end of the garden.

I hung sheets and blankets on the line and across the bushes behind the house to air them. I'd brought bread and milk and three slices of ham for my tea. While I ate, I wondered what it would be like to live here with Paul. Would he be happy in such a quiet place, away from the streets of Leamington, among accents that are as flat as the Curragh plain?

And then my head said, *Foolish woman! You think two days of excitement is a recipe for half a lifetime together? You think a man with his own business will leave a thriving town to live with you in isolation? Surely you don't believe he wouldn't lose interest in a month or two?*

I thought about the letter I posted on Tuesday. Had it arrived yet in Leamington? I presumed it had. My stomach churned and turned and I put aside my food.

Monday, May 14

Two letters come. One is an invitation to the wedding of my husband's niece in June. The second is from Leamington. I open the envelope and four photographs tumble out on the table. Colour photographs. One of the front of Paul's bookshop, the window frame and door painted a duck-egg blue. *The Quiet Corner Bookshop* in fancy writing on a board above the window. One of a small garden with a weeping maple in the corner. One of a country lane somewhere in England, the hedges leaning inward, and one of the street outside his shop, the early morning or late evening shadows crawling across a deserted road.

The letter runs to just three sentences: *I understand. I hope these snaps answer your questions about the where and how of my life. As to the inner life, you'll need to ask me when we meet.*

When he comes in for his supper, my husband reads the wedding invitation.

'That'll be a good day out with a fair few measures,' he says.

Wednesday, May 16

Where the river swings left, about two miles down from the lock house, there's a forest that rises high and sharp above the water. A forest of sycamore, ash, alder and beech. The branches and leaves are one umbrella above the dry earth. Sometimes I walk between the trees. But there are other days when I stand on the riverbank and stare up into the deep and distant summer forest and imagine myself brave and free enough to live there. What would it be like to disappear among the trees, to live alone in a woodland, winter and summer, and come out only at night to visit my babies' graves; to stand at the foot of the garden and watch my husband through the lit window of the kitchen; to see the light go out in his bedroom; to walk away again and leave him miles behind. A dream, a dream, a dream.

Thursday, May 17

The field behind the Little Wood has been sown with sugar beet. I think ahead to November and the ugly business of harvesting. All that muck and the roads like battlefields. But, for now, those days and weeks lie far away. In the coming months the beet fields will turn green. Their blistered leaves will spread between the drills, across the hedges from the stubbled fields and the precious bales.

In June and July, the silent countryside, like an empty quarry in the midday heat, will be flecked with swallows, close as undertakers to the ground. In the soaring days of August, the red sun, still slow to set, will turn the beet leaves to ochre.

The world turns and I stand and watch and wonder. I get lost in the colours and the smells and the change from one season to another, and my life passes by while I'm waiting for a man to come on a barge. I love the days but the days do me no favours.

Tuesday, May 22

One of the things I discovered when I first moved to this house was the tradition of the trees. To each lock house went a pair of plum and apple trees and afterwards a pair of lilac trees. I thought it a wonderful custom, one of those things that made me feel the world was right. It and the flowers from the past and the ghosts who looked after us. But, in time, none of this was enough.

One lock-keeper I heard of sowed his trees in a slump behind the house, on wet, marshy and inaccessible land. The lock-keeper at Maganey sowed a lilac and a plum on the small island where canal and river part and then join again. That island is a riot of scent and colour in June and provides a feast of fruit in autumn.

Here the trees are sown in the garden, neatly spaced on either side of the potato drills and raised beds. It wasn't always so. When we first arrived, there was only grass on the width of garden between the fruits. But my husband sowed new trees – damson and cherry. The grass disappeared, all but a small plot in the shelter of the house.

The rest became a vegetable patch with paths between the beds and drills, as neat as pins.

The first summer after we moved here, my husband tried to teach me how to swim. His hands were gentle under me and sometimes they edged up from my belly to my breasts and we'd giggle in the water and go inside and make love in the room above the garden, the big brass bed singing its own satisfying song as our bodies ran together.

That summer the sun shone long and the shadows it threw were sharp and clear, and possibility was everywhere. And when the sun began to dip that hour earlier, we sowed the daffodils, the snowdrops and the crocuses, both bent towards the earth. And afterwards, we stood inside the low stone wall admiring our handiwork and then lay down before the first fire of autumn.

I never did master the art of swimming. He became annoyed as the summer ended and I still couldn't manage to breathe between strokes.

'Only a fool won't learn to swim,' he said. 'What happens when you slip some frosty February morning while you're crossing the lock, when the planks are iced up, and there's no one here to pull you out? What happens if you're six foot from the wall and a stroke or two would take you there but all you can do is shout and drown? What then? How stupid would that be?'

But I never learned to swim – not learning became a kind of promise to myself.

Thursday, May 24

Dear Julie,

I was reading a book last night on Columbus and his adventures and I began to think of myself as an adventurer – I know the Barrow is not the Atlantic! – and this idea came to me that, even in sight of land, I feel the panic Columbus's second-in-command must have felt once he had lost the sight and sound of trees.

It's as if that man, whoever he was, lost faith in timber once it had been felled, torn root by root from the ground. As though the Niña, *the* Pinta *and the* Santa María *were less reliable because their timbers were no longer rooted in the earth.*

And then I realised it wasn't the book or Columbus or his second-in-command I was thinking about but you. I know what I want for us but not seeing you, not speaking to you, makes me lose my confidence.

I can hear you say, 'What is he talking about? He's digressing again.' And I am. What I'm trying to say is that I miss you and I can neither explain nor understand how two days could change my life but change it they did.

I have an idea and, fool that I am, I should have thought of it long ago. My shop is open Monday to Saturday from ten till six. I close, as does the town, for a half-day on Thursdays. My telephone number is on the card I put inside the Steinbeck book. Would you telephone some day? Reverse charges, of course. To hear your voice! Mornings are always quiet but, if you can, call at any time. I would be so pleased.

Yours,
Paul

Laburnum, lilac, the whitethorn bride, red poppies in the tanning corn. Imagine if these were the code words we used and each knew the meaning of the message sent.

Friday, May 25

I want to telephone. I will telephone but not today. This is a promise and it is also a possibility I wish to savour. On Tuesday I'll cycle to Carlow. I'll choose some books in the library. I'll make my way to the post office and stand in one of the kiosks there and telephone Paul.

I know the number off by heart. I've known it since I first saw it on his card. I have dreamed of ringing it from a phone box at the end of his street. I am distracted. I am delighted. I am terrified.

Tuesday, May 29

I waited until my husband had gone up the bank before I dressed, putting on my best summer frock. Fool that I am, I wanted to look well when I telephoned Paul. I put my library books in the shopping bag and secured it on the carrier of the bike and off I went, into the bright summer morning.

As I cycled, I dreamed. I dreamed that Paul and I were following paths along the banks of whatever river runs through or near Leamington. It was a summer evening and the sycamores were leaning in across the path but high above us. The earth was soft; the paths we followed were old ways, twisted and narrow. There were the hoof prints of deer in the shady places and the low, sinking sun stretched the shadows right across the width of the river. And then we found wild red euonymus in a hedge and we both laughed because it was the wrong season and Paul said, 'It must have waited patiently for us all winter and spring and into summer.' And I found myself laughing out loud as I cycled and an old man called from a field, 'It must be a good one.' I smiled, waved back at him and cycled on.

The town was Tuesday quiet. I left my bicycle outside the library, returned my books, took my time in choosing three more and then walked slowly down to the post office. It was noiseless and cool after the heat of Dublin Street. Someone had tied a donkey and cart to the post outside the door. I stepped into a booth, closed the door behind me and lifted the receiver.

'Number, please,' a voice said.

I gave the number and the town.

'You have your money ready?' the voice asked.

'I do.'

'I'll connect you so.'

Silence and then the ringing of a telephone and then a man's voice. 'The Quiet Corner Bookshop. Paul speaking.'

'Paul,' I said and there was silence.

'Julie? Are you in London?'

'No, I'm not.'

'Are you in Leamington? Are you about to walk into the shop?'

I laughed. 'No, I'm in the post office in Carlow.'

'Shall I call you back? Give me the number.'

'I have lots of money. You don't need to ring me back.'

'Well, give me the number anyway. Just in case.'

I read the number from the chart on the wall.

'How are you?' Paul asked and, before I could answer, he said, 'It's so bloody wonderful to hear you. You don't know how wonderful.'

'I'm well,' I said. 'And how are you?'

We talked for ten minutes and he made me promise I'd ring him in two weeks and he urged me, again, to come to London, to come to Leamington, to come and see him. I said I'd think about it. I promised I'd give it serious consideration.

By the time I was halfway home, I realised that, like Christmas, the phone call had brought an inevitable sense of disappointment. Nothing had changed. We were still hundreds of miles and a sea apart. I felt foolish in my best dress. I thought of the babies and I imagined their looks of disappointment and accusation that I would consider leaving them with only a drunken sot to tend their graves, and my heart felt like breaking.

Friday, June 1

Sunrise this morning was calm. I tried to raise my spirits, but since the phone call to Paul, I have felt foolish and low. Last night, before he went up to bed, my husband said, 'Are you worsening again, Julie? Are you sinking into that state again because, if you are, you'd better let me know in time?'

'I'm not,' I said. 'I'm just a bit all over the place.'

'A bit all over the place can become a long way down in jig time, as we well know.'

'I'm right as rain.'

'Good.'

The morning was clear and bright with a warm breeze. I washed and hung the bedsheets out to dry. I walked to the Low Field and gathered an armful of lilac. I left bouquets on the children's graves and put the rest in jugs in the kitchen and the bedroom. The scent of lilac always lifts my spirits.

By dinner hour the sheets were dry and I smiled when my husband came in.

'You're doing better?' he asked.

'I am. I told you, right as rain.'

'Good.'

'And there's a letter there for both of us.'

'From Margaret and Robert?'

'No, it has an Irish stamp.'

'Open it and see who it's from.'

I opened the envelope. Inside was a brief note. 'It's a reminder from your brother, not to forget the wedding on the twenty-third.'

'Does he think I'm a fool? Didn't we reply to the invitation?'

'We did.'

'The stook.'

In the late afternoon, a Lazarus wind rose at speed, hauling its shroud across the skies, trampling the blue. It reeked of a cold and wintry greed, as though this morning's heat was a dream, something short-lived. Maybe it was. Maybe the summer is over before it's begun. I stood at the gable end of the house and listened to the birds sing. They trust in life despite its brevity but you are absent my true, my treasured, my longed-for lover.

Thursday, June 7

For the past week I have worked hard at keeping myself afloat or, at worst, at hiding my darkness from my husband. I don't want to go back inside the walls of The Mental. What if Paul came and I wasn't here? What if this time there was no coming out?

There were women and men I met inside who had been in and out a couple of times but each committal was like another hammer blow that nailed them to the cross until, after three or four stays, there was no leaving. I knew by their eyes that the fight had gone out of them, so, no matter what it takes, I won't go back. I am not mad. I am sad and desperate and lonely, but I am not mad.

Friday, June 8

This morning a letter came from Leamington.

Dear Julie,

I hope you will telephone this week. Hearing your voice was the most wonderful thing.

I had intended writing sooner but the father of my young friend who took his life earlier this year was quite ill and I spent a lot of my time ferrying his wife to and from the hospital in Warwick. Thankfully, he is now on the mend and is expected home tomorrow.

How can I ever persuade you to come to England? The country is not all about London. This part of the world is very beautiful. I know you'd love it. But I do know how difficult a break it would be for you.

I'm planning on coming to Ireland in August or September – is there a <u>better</u> time from your point of view? I'll hire a barge again. How could I not? And I know things may not fall as favourably this time but I live in hope, just as I live in hope of your coming here.

But, even if you are not here, if that isn't possible, you will always be here, but only if you keep faith and expect my presence too. On the next street you walk along in Carlow, in the next telephone call, on the next silent road you cycle, in the carriage of a train, in the rising wind, in the falling rain, in times of celebration, in times of flowers and soil, in your late-night kitchen, in the first light, at dusk, among the water irises, in flesh, the next time you shudder in the cold, the next time you shudder, in the shouted reproach, in the whispered now, in the word that comes out as almost silence but is surrender, in life, in circumstance, in the moment after waking while the dream remains, in the catch in your throat, in the habitual, in the surprising, in instants of hopelessness, in moments of acceptance, at the times when you dare to imagine, in the countryside when you walk, in surrogate intimacy, in belief, in never listening to what they urge, in love, in love, in love.

Paul

His words, as unexpected as the sudden fall of gravel in the summer quarry. I am happy. I am saddened.

Monday, June 11

Last night I had another dream that wasn't really a dream but a reliving of the past.

The unborn I had called with names he scorned each time my belly grew. The first I imagined a boy and suggested the name Uinseann. The second I imagined a girl and suggested the name Fiadh.

'What kind of names are they?' he asked. 'We'd be laughed out of the parish.'

And afterwards, when they were buried, he said: 'Did it ever cross your mind, woman, that naming children that early might have brought down the wrath of God on you? With all your books, did you never read that pride is a sin? Pride, envy, gluttony, sloth ... did they not teach them out in whatever hedge-school you went to? Wasn't it pride that led to Satan falling out of heaven? Maybe your father set you reading the wrong books but, sure, pride must be in that dictionary of yours, too.'

The ones who came full term, the girl and the boy, we gave them solid names but without imagination.

Wednesday, June 13

I wrote today to Paul. I told him I was looking forward to seeing him. I told him I would manage, somehow, to see and spend time with him when he comes here. I told him Sundays are good days because my husband is away drinking for most of the day. More than that I didn't say, even though I wanted to, because promises can break and hearts with them.

Tonight my husband took his good suit from the wardrobe and put it on.

'You might check the buttons and give it a spruce-up for the wedding,' he said.

I told him I would.

I washed my own best dress and tomorrow I'll hang his suit and my coat in the orchard to air. The wedding is in Kilkenny. Already, he has booked the hackney car to take us there and back. The last time I was in a hackney car was thirteen months ago, on my way home from The Mental. Which is the better journey?

Sometimes I imagine what a heart breaking must be like. I don't want my heart to break. All I want is for it to continue its mundane task of loving me. At night, I lie awake and talk to the beating pump in my breast. I say things that sound like prayers. *In you I place my faith, don't toss that trust away. Keep beating while you can. Sing out, sing out, insane with a living, charitable song. Oh heart, just beat and beat and beat again.*

Tuesday, June 19

A short letter from Leamington.

Julie,

If you can telephone me next week – reverse charges, I insist – I will have the dates of my holiday in Ireland. You can't imagine how I look forward to seeing you and being with you again.

I look in the mirror and what I see is a woman who has aged so much in a year. And I think about this house and I imagine his house. I dream of climbing the narrow, winding stair from shop to living quarters. No field of little ghosts beyond the window. No trees, I imagine. Only a tiny garden and the walls of other houses. Could I live in such a place? I consider digging the tiny bones or what's left of them from the earth and bringing them with me to Moone. Burying them in the garden of the house where I was born. The house I lived in. The house that is my home.

Tonight, as if he'd read my mind, my husband sits across the supper table from me and says: 'The sooner you sell that house in Moone, the better. It won't benefit from another winter without being lived in. We could buy a field or two with maybe a cottage that needs doing up, with a bit of land. Get out of this place, away from the water. We'd both be better off.'

I want to tell him I have no intention of selling my home, but something in the way his tone changes as he talks makes me hear, again, the deep sadness and bitterness he feels at being tied to lock gates and barges and the rising and falling of the water.

'I'll think about it,' I say and I feel bad for misleading him. I'm the only one who can get him out of this place and this job, but only by handing him everything I own.

'I'm just saying,' he says and his voice is that of the little boy.

I pity him.

Sunday, June 24

He brought me to his niece's wedding yesterday. I really didn't want to go but he said it would be expected. How sadly glad I am.

'I want them to know things is normal, back to normal. They don't know what happened to you but in case they did ....' he said. He talks too much sometimes. 'I want them to see it for themselves, bury all them fuckin' rumours in the bottom of a hole for once and for all.'

What he really meant was he wanted me to verify his lies about my being away minding my father for five months. He wanted me to satisfy his family's uncertainties by turning up and letting them see that I was *normal.* As if it mattered, as if anyone, other than himself, gives a twopenny damn.

He had been drinking on Friday afternoon. 'Gettin' oiled up for the day ahead,' he said. When he got home from the town, he coached me on what I was to say and how I was to answer any questions that might be thrown my way. As if any of his cousins or brothers could concoct a question that I couldn't answer. I knew damn well that if they thought of me at all, gave my life any consideration, they were glad they weren't married to me. And if, as rumour doubtless had it, I was *suffering with the nerves*, it wasn't their problem.

'Once they see you, the job will be Oxo.'

'Why would they be concerned with me when they never were in the past?'

'Word has a way of leakin' out when people are senseless. News has a way of slippin' out,' he said. 'But don't you worry, I'll be there lookin' after you. Amn't I always?'

Late in the evening, after the meal and the speeches and the dancing and the drinking, I overheard my husband in conversation with his brother. He didn't realise I was within earshot.

He leaned over and spoke quietly but my ears are attuned to even his whispers. With drink taken, he cannot be quiet. 'I sank each of them, two heavy rocks and two jute sacks, so that by the time the jute was rotted there'd be only the bones left to drift.'

It might have been pups or kittens he was talking about but I knew.

Early this morning I went down to the bank of the river and looked out over the low expanse of water and wondered where, if anywhere, my children are. I thought of wading out into the place where the water is fast and deep, the channel that runs its secret way from the rising of the river to its loss in the sea. I imagined lying back and letting the waters close over me. I thought of how I might, in the last moments of consciousness or the first of unconsciousness, see my children again and travel with them between the water irises and under the bowing willows until, by moonlight, we were swept out into the after-world of the ocean. But then I imagined my husband and the bargemen bullocking my body ashore, and people's sympathy for him, and his certainty that, at last, I had proven myself insane.

I turned away and walked up the hill and off into the Little Wood and then on and on through the day.

Across fields I've never walked before. I found another river – a stream, really – that flows into the Barrow. The fresh poppies were bleeding along the headlands and the corn and the cattle were motionless beneath a clear, hot sky. I passed children playing in a garden and strangers walking in fields. One man stopped to bid me the time of day; he lifted his hat as I passed and I thought of my father. I walked for miles and hours, and by the time I got back, it was supper hour and I had to rush a meal onto the table. I didn't want my husband to know how long I'd been gone. He'd ask why and my fear was that I'd tell him. Tell him what I'd overheard at the wedding. Tell him what had crossed my mind when I woke first thing this morning. Tell him what I'd wondered as I walked. Tell him what, finally, I'd decided on doing.

Monday, June 25

I have put everything in order. I have washed and reset the crockery on the dresser. I have left what clothes I don't need in the chest of drawers. I have piled the freshly cut logs in the lean-to shed at the side of the house. Everything is ordered, just the way I like it. Since the children went away to England to work, it's easier to keep things in the places where they belong.

There's a rowdy joy in the way children leave things where they drop and a quiet joy in the collecting of these things after they have fallen asleep. I always loved that hour when the house went quiet and I could gather their books and toys and pencils and put some order on them, at least for that night. But there is a quieter – dare I say deeper? – joy in ordering a house and knowing it will continue that way for as long as for ever takes.

There is little I can say that is positive about my husband beyond that fact that he, too, likes order, so much so that when he dug the sham and empty graves, he dug them side by side, each one the same dimension, and marked their outlines carefully with stones. And tomorrow, after all these years, I will scatter the stones into the waters of the Barrow, throw them as far out into the little rippling waves as I can manage and watch them sink through the radiant summer liquid that is always yet never the same.

On the day of my Confirmation, my father gave me my dictionary.

'The best book you'll ever read,' he said.

Every day I read a page of that book and memorise new words, remember old words that were memorised once and lost and found again.

My husband is jealous of my words.

'Big words give people notions about themselves,' he told me once. And yet, whenever he finds a word that sits comfortably in his mouth, he'll use it time and time again. *Incarcerated* and *emergency* and *languid*, though he pronounces emergency as *emigrency* and he thinks languid means lazy. 'He's a languid bastard,' he'll say about one of the bargemen after he's seen them through the lock gates. 'A languid bastard that wouldn't raise a sweat in an *emigrency*.'

I never contradicted him because, if I did, he'd have sneered and asked the same jaded question: 'Is that what it says in your father's ould word book? Isn't it a quare thing that a man so fond of words ended up ploughin' the land and leadin' horses in and out of stables all his life?'

Tomorrow, I'll scatter the stones. And then I'll put my suitcase on the carrier of my bike and cycle to Carlow. From there, I'll telephone Paul and tell him that I've left this place for ever. I'll invite him to visit me in Moone when he comes on his holiday. I'll tell him that, yes, I'll visit him in Leamington but I won't live there. I'll live my own life in my own home and, if he cares to visit, he'll be welcome and, beyond that, we'll see what the world may bring.

www.ingramcontent.com/pod-product-compliance
Lightning Source LLC
LaVergne TN
LVHW100922110826
845155LV00036B/52

* 9 7 8 1 8 4 3 5 1 9 7 2 0 *